dorian

Also from EATMS Productions

Books on power, survival, women's autonomy, and the systems shaping modern America.

Nonfiction

Billionaires, Capitalism, and Power

Evil and the Mountain Ungreed
Self Help for American Billionaires
Selfish Steve and the Ivory Tower
Tariffs, Taxes, & Face-Eating Leopards
Ban Billionaires: Fascism Fix

Fascism, Religion, and Cultural Control

Self Help for the Manosphere
Fascism 2025
Fascism & the Perverts & the Greed Virus
Christian Fascism Marriage Book
Tyranny, Table Manners, & Tiramisu

Guides for Women's Autonomy and Protection

How to Survive in Post-America as a Woman
Project 2025 American Drag
4B – Burn, Ban, Boycott, Build
4B OG – So No Go GYN
I'm Glad He's Dead

Analysis of Authoritarian Project 2025

Project 2025: The Blueprint
Project 2025: The List
Project 2025, Christian Dumb Dumbs, & The Republican Agenda
Fascism, Project 2025, & The Pinkprint

Modern Rewrites for Women

Stoic Principles Reimagined
Siddhartha Reimagined
The Prince Reimagined for Women
The Art of War Reimagined for Women
The Jungle Reimagined
The Constitution Reimagined for Women

Machine Learning Series

AI, Bitcoin, Nostr for Women
AI, Safety, & Security for Women
AI, Anxiety, & Health for Women
AI, Kids, & Family Safety for Women
AI, Creativity, & Personal Expression for Women
AI, Independent Work, & Parallel Power for Women

Social Systems Series

Emotional Labor for Women
Household Power for Women
Workplace Power for Women
Medical Bias for Women
Aging Systems for Women
Recovery Systems for Women

Fiction

Dystopian Stories of Resistance and Collapse

Propaganda Paige & the Missing Prosperity
Propaganda Paige & the TIDE Manifesto
Propaganda Paige & the Shadow Cartographers
Propaganda Paige & the Prosperity Alliance
Propaganda Paige & the Shattered Truth
Propaganda Paige & the Rising TIDE
Propaganda Paige & the Last Bastion
Propaganda Paige & the Dawn of Prosperity
Project 2025: Dorian — The Last Men
Project 2025: Boy — A Last Men Novel

project 2025
dorian
the last men

Archive 1

by
Mary Schiele

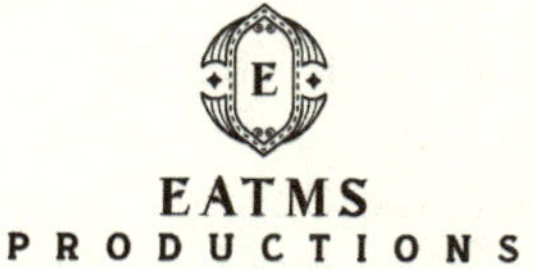

EATMS
PRODUCTIONS

This title is part of an ongoing body of work. All EATMS Productions titles, across all series, authors, and formats, are components of a single connected project.

ISBN: 978-1-966014-15-7

Cover, interior design, interior prints by: Esme Mees

eatms@pm.me
www.eatms.me

Printed in the United States of America.

Thoughts and Prayers.

— Cowards

Table of Contents

ACT I

THE FALL OF MAN
(THE FLOW BEGINS)

1
The Last Day of Power

Dorian Thorne St. Claire had never woken up to silence before. Silence, in his world, meant failure. It meant someone, somewhere, wasn't doing their job. From the moment he opened his eyes, his life was a symphony of control, security reports, pre-market briefings, political strategies being enacted in real time by people whose entire careers revolved around keeping him informed. And yet, this morning, as he stretched lazily in his bed, something felt distinctly wrong. No alerts. No messages. No reassuring hum of his empire functioning as it should.

The stillness had a weight to it, pressing into the room, wrapping around him like a phantom. His fingers reached for his phone, lifting it from the nightstand with the ease of a man who had never needed to doubt its presence. The screen didn't light up. He tapped it. Nothing. Pressed the power button. No response. The tension in his chest sharpened. His encrypted network was designed to prevent outages. Fail-safes on top of fail-safes. Nothing could cut him off. And yet, here he was.

Swinging his legs over the bed, he padded across the marble floor, glancing at the sprawling skyline through the floor-to-ceiling windows. New York still gleamed, golden in the early morning sun. But something was off. Too still. The streets below, usually a mess of honking horns and impatient drivers, were eerily empty. No cabs darting through lanes, no endless foot traffic weaving across intersections. A deep, unnatural quiet pressed against the glass.

Dorian's stomach tightened as he turned toward the control panel embedded in the wall, pressing his palm to the biometric scanner. The interface flickered once, then dimmed. No signal. No access. The tension in his spine solidified into a slow, creeping unease. He

moved toward the oversized in-wall screen near his desk, voice-commanding it on. The screen hesitated, then came alive with a burst of static. His pulse quickened. A system-wide failure at this scale was impossible. His empire had redundancies, levels of protection against everything from cyberattacks to government interference. This wasn't a glitch. This wasn't an outage. This was something else.

The static cleared. A message appeared, stark against the black screen. Simple. Uncompromising.

"You had your turn. It's over. The Flow has begun."

For the first time in his life, Dorian hesitated. He had faced market crashes, global scandals, political takedowns engineered by lesser men, and walked away untouched. But this? This was different. This wasn't a threat. It was a statement.

His hand moved to the remote, flipping through channels with growing urgency. Every screen displayed the same message. No news, no government announcements, no emergency broadcasts. A total blackout, except for those nine words. He turned back to his desk, fingers flying across the keyboard, attempting to override the block. Nothing. No command functioned. No system responded. He had been locked out of his own world.

A slow exhale left his lips, measured, controlled. This wasn't an attack. It wasn't a hack. This was real.

His breath quickened, but he forced himself to remain composed. He'd spent his life dealing with crises. The difference was, he'd always been the one with the upper hand. He pushed away from his desk and strode toward his bedroom closet. If something was happening, if some unfathomable shift had begun, he would meet it on his terms. He yanked open the doors, grabbing for the tailored navy suit hanging in the center. Clothing mattered. Image mattered. The world could be burning outside, but Dorian Thorne St. Claire would still look like the man who owned it.

The simple act of dressing steadied him, as it always had. He adjusted the cuffs of his crisp white shirt, slid into the jacket, and smoothed a hand over his hair. Control was a matter of perception. If he looked the part, the rest would follow.

A sudden, deep vibration rattled the glass walls. A sound like distant thunder, low and menacing, rolled through the air. He turned sharply back to the window. The streets were still empty, but the silence had changed. It wasn't just the absence of sound; it was the presence of something else. Something waiting.

His fingers curled into fists. He needed more information.

Crossing back to his desk, he activated his private surveillance network. The screens flickered again, but this time they complied. The security feeds pulled up a grid of live footage, inside his building, the street below, the private garage, the secondary penthouse elevator. He watched each frame intently, his sharp gaze scanning for movement. Nothing.

And then, he saw them.

Two figures, moving through the empty lobby below. Women. Dressed in black, tactical, precise. Their strides were smooth, unhurried. Not panicked. Not uncertain. They were moving with purpose. With confidence.

His pulse spiked.

He adjusted the cameras, zooming in. The lobby, the entrance, the hallway leading to his private elevator, they were already inside. His security should have intercepted them. The guards should have been at their posts. But there was no one. Just the two figures, moving closer.

Dorian's stomach tightened.

He reached for his desk drawer, fingers moving toward the biometric lock on the hidden compartment where his gun was stored. He pressed his thumb to the scanner. Access denied.

His jaw locked. He tried again. The red light flashed.

Access denied.

He exhaled sharply, shifting back to the surveillance feeds. One of the women had stopped. She lifted her head slightly, as if sensing him watching.

A message blinked onto the screen, overriding the feeds, filling every monitor with a single line:

"You don't need those anymore, John-1688A7-ICK2F ."

His breath caught. The realization slammed into him all at once. The Flow wasn't coming. It was already here.

For the first time in his life, Dorian Thorne St. Claire was not in control.

Dorian's heartbeat pounded in his ears as he stared at the screen. His own security system, the one he had personally overseen and layered with redundancies, had locked him out. The realization came slow and thick, like syrup sliding down glass, his power was slipping through his fingers, and there was nothing he could do to stop it. His body moved on instinct, pushing back from the desk, his chair scraping against the polished floor. He crossed the vast space of his penthouse, heading for the secondary command panel built into the wall near the elevator. His fingerprint should override the system, reset everything, restore his control.

It didn't. The screen blinked once and then died.

A ripple of unease spread through his chest. The protocol was designed to be foolproof. It had been engineered for him, built into the very fabric of his fortress. No one outside his inner circle had access. No one should have been able to override his authority. He pressed his palm against the panel again, this time harder, as though brute force might change the outcome. Still nothing. The house was dead.

He turned sharply, walking back toward the security feeds, his pulse accelerating. The figures on the screen were closer now, moving through the empty lobby without hesitation, their confidence terrifying in its casualness. They were not breaking in. They were not sneaking. They were walking in as if they owned the place.

His hand hovered over the control panel, his mind flipping through options. Every exit in the building required his personal access. The elevators were locked without his code. There was no conceivable way anyone could reach his level without explicit permission. Yet, the cameras showed a different story. They were coming. And they were coming for him.

A flicker of movement on another screen caught his attention. He tapped into the street view. Fifth Avenue lay in eerie silence, the city's usual roar reduced to a whisper. No honking, no screeching tires, no rush of people on their way to work. His stomach twisted. He had seen New York in many states, blizzards shutting down traffic, power outages turning streets into black holes, even the rare moments in the early morning when the city still seemed half-asleep. But this wasn't sleep. This was something else. This was absence.

A dull thud echoed through the penthouse, faint but distinct. He turned toward the sound, his muscles coiling tight. It had come from the hallway. The only hallway leading to his penthouse. He moved toward the door, his steps measured, forcing his breath to slow. He pressed his ear against the cold surface, listening. Silence. He adjusted the settings on the wall panel, activating the last remaining internal security sensor. A map of the penthouse layout spread across the screen, highlighting movement in red. Two figures. Five feet from his door.

His throat tightened. He wasn't ready to accept what this meant. He wasn't ready to believe that the same world that had worshipped him just yesterday had suddenly decided to erase him. But the facts lined up, undeniable and cold. He was no longer untouchable.

His first instinct was to run, but where? He reached for his phone again, useless. He had to think. His private elevator required biometric access. It was programmed to recognize his DNA, his retinal scan, his voice. It should have been the one place no one else could reach. But he had seen the way they moved in the lobby, the calculated precision of their steps. They weren't guessing. They weren't searching. They were executing a plan.

Another sound. This time, softer. More deliberate. A shift in pressure against the door. The knowledge settled in his bones. They were testing it. Measuring its resistance.

The overwhelming quiet of the city, the locked-out systems, the approaching shadows, it all converged into one undeniable truth. The world had moved on without him.

He backed away from the door, his breath steady but shallow. He had always known the tides would shift eventually. He had spent his career ensuring they never turned against him. But this wasn't a shift. This was a flood. A force bigger than anything he could have anticipated. He had controlled governments, manipulated markets, dictated narratives that shaped entire elections. But now, he was just another man in a suit, standing in his own tomb.

A light flickered from the desk. The screen adjusted itself, pixels realigning, static morphing into something new. He turned, pulse hammering, as a video feed emerged. It wasn't the city. It wasn't his security system. It was him. A live feed of himself standing in his penthouse, staring at the screen.

His breath hitched.

They were watching him.

And they wanted him to know it.

The screen adjusted again. A new message replaced the image. This time, it wasn't a command. It was an invitation.

"Open the door, John-1688A7-ICK2F ."

Dorian's pulse pounded in his ears as he took another step back from the screen. He felt, for the first time in his life, like prey. He had spent decades cultivating power, positioning himself above the rules that governed lesser men. He had been untouchable. And yet, as he stood there, watching his own reflection flicker on the screen, being observed by unseen forces, he knew that something had shifted. The world had changed overnight, and he had not changed with it.

The words on the screen, open the door, John-1688A7-ICK2F , burned into his retinas. He had been assigned a new name, stripped of his legacy before the fight had even begun. That alone told him what he needed to know. This wasn't a hostile takeover with demands, not a negotiation he could manipulate. His wealth, his status, his influence, all of it was meaningless now. The certainty of it pressed against his ribs, making his breaths shallow and uneven.

He turned away from the screen and forced himself to think. If the security systems had been compromised, if the surveillance feeds were no longer his to control, then he had to assume every pathway out of this penthouse was also compromised. His private elevator would be the first thing they locked down. The stairwell was an option, but descending seventy-five floors would make him a sitting target. His rooftop helipad, his last resort, required clearance codes that he no longer had access to. Every exit had been sealed before he had even begun looking for one.

His fingers twitched at his sides. He hated the feeling of inertia, of waiting. He had always been a man of action, the kind who dictated terms rather than reacted to them. The idea that he was meant to stand here, obediently awaiting capture, made something hot and furious coil inside his chest. He moved back toward his desk, fingers flying over the touchpad, bypassing the usual interfaces, digging into the root systems buried beneath the surface software. He had spent millions ensuring that his digital footprint could never be erased. Somewhere, buried deep, there had to be a way back in.

But as quickly as he tried to maneuver through backdoor entries, the system erased itself, sealing every path as though it had anticipated his next move before he had even made it. His own digital infrastructure had been turned against him, mirroring the cold, inevitable collapse of his physical power.

A sharp noise, metal shifting against metal, sent ice down his spine. The door. They were still testing it, still measuring its strength against whatever tools they had brought. His mind ticked through the possibilities. They weren't rushing, which meant they knew they had time. They weren't worried about him escaping. That, more than anything, told him exactly how much control he had lost.

His gaze flicked toward the far side of the penthouse, where the glass doors led to his rooftop terrace. He strode toward them, his mind moving faster now, forcing his body to fall into action. The terrace connected to the adjacent building, an older structure that lacked the same state-of-the-art security he had prided himself on. If he could scale across the ledge, reach that building's maintenance access, he might be able to slip out unnoticed.

The second his hands pressed against the glass, the cityscape stretched out before him like an open grave. New York had always been a thing of noise and motion, a city that never stood still. And yet, there was nothing. No people. No movement. The skyline shimmered, eerily untouched, as though someone had frozen time itself.

His stomach twisted. It wasn't just his building. It wasn't just him. The entire city had been silenced.

The terrace door wouldn't budge. He checked the mechanism. Locked. Another override. Another layer of control stripped from him without warning. He slammed his palm against the glass, a brief moment of frustration cracking through his usually impenetrable composure.

A new sound filled the room. Not metal against metal this time. Something softer. A slow, deliberate beep. He turned his head sharply, eyes snapping back to the control panels near the elevator. The emergency override panel had been activated. The system was preparing to unlock the door.

They were done waiting.

Dorian moved. His body responded faster than his mind, pushing him back across the penthouse, his vision tunneling in on the emergency weapons vault embedded in the wall. He didn't care that the system had denied him access earlier. He needed to try again. He reached the scanner, pressed his palm to the pad. Nothing. He tried again, willing it to recognize him. The red light blinked once.

Access denied.

His teeth clenched. He was running out of time. He turned, scanning the room for anything he could use as a weapon, anything that might buy him the precious seconds he needed to find another exit. The penthouse, once a fortress, now felt like a gilded cage. Every luxury he had built into it, every touch of opulence meant to remind him of his dominion, now served as a mockery of the power he no longer had.

A hiss of hydraulics sounded from the front door. The locks were releasing. His time was up.

Dorian forced himself to breathe, to slow the panic crawling up his spine. If they wanted him to break, they wouldn't get the satisfaction. He had spent his life outmaneuvering his enemies. This moment would be no different. He straightened his suit jacket, adjusted his cuffs. Whatever happened next, he would meet it standing.

The door slid open.

He exhaled, steady. Then, he turned to face them.

Dorian stood motionless as the door slid open, revealing the two women who had walked through his fortress as though it were already theirs. They stepped inside with an air of complete authority, their expressions unreadable, their movements precise. They weren't armed, at least not visibly, and that told him everything he needed to know. They didn't need weapons. Theirs was a power that came from absolute certainty.

One of them, tall, with dark, calculating eyes, tilted her head slightly as she studied him. The other, slightly shorter, exuded an air of quiet command, the kind that did not need to be spoken aloud to be understood. Neither hesitated. They had already decided how this moment would play out, and Dorian was merely catching up.

He clenched his jaw, refusing to speak first. There was still power in silence, even now. He would not offer them the satisfaction of watching him crack. He had built an empire on understanding leverage, on knowing when to strike and when to wait. Yet standing here, stripped of his networks, his security, his options, he had nothing left to bargain with.

The taller woman finally spoke. "Dorian Thorne St. Claire." She said his name as though it was a historical artifact, something already obsolete. "You understand what's happening." It wasn't a question. It was a statement of fact. He held her gaze, refusing to give her anything.

The shorter woman stepped forward. "You should consider yourself lucky," she said, her voice smooth, measured. "Most men in your position didn't get this much courtesy."

Dorian exhaled slowly. "Courtesy?" His voice was even, but the weight of the moment pressed down on him. "You walk into my home, shut down my city, erase my name from my own systems, and call this courtesy?"

The taller woman let out a small, almost amused breath. "We could have done this while you were sleeping. You'd have never even had the moment to process it." She gestured around them. "Instead, we gave you time to understand. We let you wake up in your world one last time, before it became ours."

Something cold settled in his gut. This wasn't chaos. This wasn't a coup of screaming mobs and desperate, last-ditch resistance. This was order. This was structure. Every step had been measured, accounted for, planned with a precision he would have respected under different circumstances.

He glanced toward the security feeds, still displaying the frozen cityscape. "How?" he asked, not because he expected them to answer, but because the sheer scale of the operation demanded recognition.

The shorter woman answered anyway. "Planning. Coordination. Understanding that real power isn't held by those who take, but by those who can cut off what is taken." She looked around the penthouse, her expression unreadable. "You built this world on control. You just never imagined what would happen if someone else understood it better than you."

Dorian felt his throat tighten, but he masked it well. This wasn't just about him. This wasn't just about power. This was about something deeper, something that had been set in motion long before this moment. He had underestimated them. All of them.

The taller woman stepped closer now, closing the space between them. "You already know there's no way out," she said. "So don't make this harder than it has to be."

His hands curled into fists at his sides, but there was no point in posturing. They were right. There was no way out. Not through money, not through influence, not through force. His world had already fallen.

He swallowed once, hard, before finally speaking again. "What now?"

The shorter woman's lips curled slightly, not quite a smirk, not quite sympathy. "Now?" She turned slightly, as though considering. "Now you stop being Dorian Thorne St. Claire."

The words landed like a hammer.

He had known it was coming, had seen it in the erasure of his accounts, the blacked-out screens, the message calling him John-1688A7-ICK2F . And yet hearing it said aloud, final and absolute, hit him in a way nothing else had.

The taller woman reached into her pocket, pulling out a thin, black device, no larger than a credit card. She held it up, pressed her thumb to the surface, and a holographic display illuminated between them. His face appeared on the screen, but beneath it, where his name should have been, there was only a string of numbers.

The proof of his erasure, more real than anything else. He stared at it, and for the first time, a small fissure of something close to fear cracked through the carefully built exterior he had maintained his entire life.

The shorter woman caught it, her gaze sharp. “You don’t have to fight it,” she said, voice lower now, almost patient. “It’s already done.”

Dorian swallowed, pushing the fear down, deep enough that it wouldn’t show. “And if I refuse?”

The taller woman pocketed the device again. “Then we proceed with Option B.”

He didn’t need to ask what that meant.

His body was still, but inside, his mind raced through the implications. Option A: compliance. Submission. Survival, if it could be called that. Option B: the alternative. He didn’t need a breakdown of what that entailed. He had seen enough governments collapse, enough regimes shift, enough opposition removed to know what it meant when the people in power gave you a choice without really giving you one.

He let out a slow, steady breath. “I’ll walk.”

The shorter woman nodded once. “Good.”

She turned, moving toward the door, expecting him to follow. The taller woman lingered for a moment longer, watching him. Studying him. “You’re going to realize soon,” she said, “that the worst part isn’t losing power. It’s realizing you were never as powerful as you thought.”

Dorian didn’t answer. He had nothing left to say.

With measured steps, he followed them out of the penthouse, into a world where he no longer existed.

2
The Rivers Move In

Dorian walked between them, each step measured, forced. His mind was a battlefield of calculations, each thought dissecting the few remaining options he might have. None of them led to anything but a dead end. The elevator ride down from his penthouse was silent. Not because there was nothing to say, but because there was nothing left to argue. The women flanking him had already won. The world had already been rewritten. He was merely stepping into its new reality.

The descent was slow. Too slow. He had taken this ride countless times before, always impatient for what waited below, meetings, deals, appearances, decisions that shaped markets and governments. But now, time stretched thin, forcing him to sit inside his own head, to wrestle with what had happened, what was still happening. He glanced at the mirrored walls of the elevator. The reflection staring back at him looked the same. The tailored suit, the expensive watch, the sharp angles of his face that had graced magazine covers, political forums, and corporate profiles. And yet, none of it mattered. Not anymore.

The doors slid open into a lobby that no longer belonged to him. The space had been altered in a way he hadn't thought possible in the span of mere hours. Gone were the towering floral arrangements, the gilded fixtures, the polished arrogance of wealth designed to intimidate those beneath it. Instead, the air felt stripped bare, intentional. As if anything unnecessary had already been removed, discarded along with the men who once walked these halls.

The silence was thicker here. In the absence of security, of personal aides, of the ever-present machine of his empire running in the background, the weight of it pressed down on him. The two women stepped forward, forcing him to keep pace, leading him toward the street outside. The glass doors parted smoothly, revealing the waiting city.

Except it wasn't waiting for him. It was waiting for them.

Dorian's breath slowed as his gaze swept the scene beyond the doors. The streets, once carved out for men like him, now belonged to something else entirely. Women moved with purpose, methodical and uninterrupted. There was no chaos, no hesitation. Every motion was a statement. A new order had replaced the old overnight, yet it had been so meticulously planned that there was no trace of rebellion, no smoldering ruins left in its wake. Only efficiency.

He stepped outside, and the heat of the morning hit his skin, the smell of the city, usually a blend of gasoline, ambition, and desperation, now somehow cleaner, as if it too had shed its past. A fleet of matte-black vehicles lined the curb, unmarked, seamless in design. He recognized the style immediately. Not government-issued. Something else. Something outside the bounds of what he had once controlled.

The shorter woman, the one who had spoken less but commanded just as much presence, gestured toward one of the vehicles. "Get in."

For a moment, he hesitated. Not out of defiance, but out of instinct. His entire life had been dictated by control, by the ability to set his own course. Now, for the first time, he was a passenger in someone else's plan. He moved toward the vehicle, sliding into the backseat without another word. The doors shut with an airtight finality.

The interior was cool, the scent inside sharp and unfamiliar. The car pulled away from the curb with smooth precision, and for the first time since he had woken up that morning, Dorian realized that this was not temporary. There was no one coming to rescue him, no plan unfolding behind the scenes to reclaim what was his. He was in transit, not toward a negotiation, but toward whatever version of existence they had decided he was now fit for.

The streets moved past the windows, but they were not the streets he had known. Billboards that had once been filled with campaign ads, luxury brands, and the faces of men just like him were stripped bare or replaced entirely. The faces that looked down at the city were not those of the past. They belonged to the new architects, the ones who had built something underneath the rot of the old world and waited for the right moment to surface.

The vehicle turned, moving away from the financial district, heading toward a part of the city that Dorian rarely acknowledged outside of land deals and zoning meetings. He felt his jaw tighten. There were no mistakes in their movements. Wherever they were taking him, it had been decided long before today.

The woman beside him glanced his way, and for the first time since the door of his penthouse had opened, he saw something in her expression that wasn't calculation. It wasn't sympathy, either. It was something simpler.

"You're processing it," she said, more an observation than a question.

Dorian exhaled, slow and measured. "I don't have much of a choice, do I?"

Her lips twitched slightly, but she said nothing. They both knew the answer.

The vehicle moved with a smoothness that felt unnatural, gliding through the city without the familiar jostle of potholes, sudden stops, or erratic lane changes. Dorian sat stiffly, his fingers curled against his knee, resisting the urge to check his watch, a habit, a relic of control he still clung to. Time, however, was no longer his to command. He stared out the tinted window, taking in the landscape as they passed through the city's veins, deeper into a world that had already been reshaped without his consent.

Gone were the towering billboards featuring the faces of men like him, their power immortalized in digital pixels, selling the illusion of permanence. In their place were sharp, minimalist declarations, words in bold, uncompromising letters. *Your turn is over. The Flow is absolute. Order begins where corruption ends.* The messages were not defaced, not vandalized, these were intentional, state-sanctioned proclamations, displayed with the same authority once wielded by campaign ads and corporate branding. They had not erased the old world in fire. They had rewritten it in certainty.

Dorian swallowed against the tightening in his throat. His buildings still stood, the structures he had financed, the investments that bore his name etched in steel and glass. But he knew, instinctively, that those names would not remain. He was witnessing the last echoes of a past that had been given no funeral. The future had already moved in.

The car turned off the main avenue, gliding toward a part of the city that felt unnervingly foreign despite its familiarity. The government district. Court buildings, civic centers, places of law and judgment. The realization settled in his gut like lead. They weren't taking him to a detention center. They were taking him to be processed.

The shorter woman, seated beside him with the quiet authority of someone who did not need to announce her control, finally spoke. "You should consider yourself fortunate," she said, her tone as neutral as it had been since they first entered his penthouse. "Most of your kind don't get a formal hearing."

Dorian's jaw tightened. "Is that what this is?"

She turned her head slightly, studying him. "You think you still have a say in this."

His pulse quickened. He had once been in rooms where governments were bought and sold, where policy was molded to his advantage with nothing more than the right donation, the right handshake. The idea that he would now be placed on trial like some nameless bureaucrat was almost laughable. And yet, the streets outside told him this was no temporary upheaval. The Flow had been thorough. Calculated. This was not rebellion. It was restructuring.

The vehicle came to a stop in front of a building that had once housed the Supreme Court. Its marble pillars remained, but the banners draped over them were new. The insignia of the old order had been replaced by a singular emblem, a fluid, wave-like design, stark and unyielding in its simplicity. The doors, guarded but not barricaded, opened at their arrival. There was no sense of military imposition, no display of armed force. They did not need it. The transition was already complete.

The woman beside him reached for the door handle but paused, turning back to him one last time. "You'll want to stand tall when you walk in there."

Dorian resisted the urge to scoff. It was an old instinct, one that no longer served him. Instead, he straightened his shoulders, exhaling slowly as he stepped out of the car, into the open air of his reckoning.

Inside, the building was silent save for the echo of his own footsteps against polished stone. The halls, once filled with the murmurs of clerks, attorneys, and the rustling of paperwork, now felt sterile. Functional. This was no longer a place of endless deliberation, where justice was debated and bargained for like a commodity. This was something else. A place of decisions, not arguments.

They led him through the corridors without ceremony, past doorways that no longer bore names, only numbers. He saw no other men. No familiar faces. He had spent his career surrounding himself with those who wielded power as he did, who measured their worth in influence, who had built walls around their control, believing them impenetrable. Where were they now? Were they already processed? Had they been sent elsewhere, or simply erased from this new equation entirely?

They reached a set of double doors, dark wood, unmarked. One of the guards stationed outside pressed a hand to a biometric panel. The door unlocked with an audible click.

Dorian hesitated only a fraction of a second before stepping inside.

The chamber was vast, its high ceilings lending an air of solemnity without the weight of history. This was not a court. There were no judges in robes, no jury boxes. Instead, a singular woman sat behind a broad, minimalistic desk, her presence commanding without excess. She was not dressed in judicial attire, nor in any uniform that suggested military or bureaucratic authority. She did not need to be.

He knew who she was. Everyone did.

Dominique Severin.

Her name had been whispered in the corridors of power for years, always adjacent to the movements that had now become the world itself. Where others had postured, she had calculated. Where others had incited, she had orchestrated. And now, she was sitting before him, not as a challenger to his authority, but as the one who had removed it entirely.

She regarded him with a calm that was more unnerving than outright aggression. "Dorian Thorne St. Claire," she said, as if testing the name, weighing its relevance. "You understand why you're here."

His throat was dry. "I imagine you'll tell me anyway."

A slight tilt of her head, almost an acknowledgment of his attempt to maintain dignity. "We both know your era is over. The question now is what comes next for you."

He had no response to that. Not yet.

She gestured to the seat in front of her. "Sit."

For a moment, he considered refusing. A final act of defiance, however meaningless. But he had not survived this long by making irrational moves. He sat.

She folded her hands together on the desk, leaning forward slightly. "This is not a trial," she said, voice measured. "The decisions have already been made. You are not here to argue your worth. You are here to receive your designation."

His pulse spiked. "Designation."

She nodded. "The new structure does not recognize your previous identity. You are no longer a citizen, no longer an individual with autonomous rights. You are property."

A slow, sickening realization settled in his gut. "And what exactly does that mean?"

She leaned back slightly, considering him. "It means you belong to the state now. And the state will determine how best to use you."

His hands curled into fists beneath the desk. For all the preparations he had made in his life, for all the scenarios he had accounted for, he had never once considered this.

Severin watched him for a moment longer, then picked up a tablet, tapping the screen. "Your classification will be decided shortly. Your options are limited."

Dorian exhaled slowly, suppressing the rising tide of anger threatening to overtake him. He had spent his life deciding fates. Now, his own would be decided for him.

Severin's gaze didn't waver. "I suggest you prepare yourself, John-1688A7-ICK2F ."

He didn't flinch, but inside, something cracked.

This was no longer his world.

And he was no longer a man.

Dorian sat in the cold, impersonal chair, his back rigid against the weight of the words that had just been spoken. Property. The term settled over him like a thick fog, clouding everything he had ever known about himself. It was impossible, yet here he was, being reclassified by a government that no longer recognized him as a man. He had spent his entire life making decisions, setting the course for others. Now, he was simply an asset to be assigned, a problem to be sorted.

Dominique Severin remained impassive, watching him with the calm assurance of someone who had done this before, who had sat in that chair and seen countless others just like him, men who had once ruled, now reduced to raw materials in a system designed for their elimination. She tapped on the tablet again, and the silence between them stretched, thick and unbearable. He resisted the urge to break it. He would not give her the satisfaction of desperation, not yet.

Eventually, she spoke. "There are three primary classifications under the new order," she said, her voice as even as it had been since he entered the chamber. "Labor, entertainment, or disposal." She set the tablet down, folding her hands over it. "Labor is straightforward. You'll be assigned to a work sector, given a set of duties. No privileges, no autonomy, but you serve a function. Entertainment is… selective. It depends on demand. Some men have proven useful in this regard, but that is not a decision you make. And then there's disposal." She paused, letting the word sink in. "That is reserved for those who serve no purpose."

Dorian forced himself to breathe evenly. He had spent years at the top of the world, moving through circles where men decided which industries lived and died, who was granted power and who was stripped of it. To hear those same metrics applied to him now, as though he were livestock being sorted at a slaughterhouse, sent a sharp pulse of something dangerously close to fear through his veins. He gritted his teeth. "And which am I?"

Severin tilted her head slightly, as though she had been expecting the question. "You'll be classified, officially, within the hour. But let's be honest, your profile doesn't lend itself to labor."

The implication was clear. Men like him, men who had spent their lives in luxury, who had never worked a real day in their lives, were of no use in the labor force. The thought of physical exertion, of being forced into some factory or agricultural field like a common worker, was so far from his reality that he couldn't fully wrap his mind around it. But the alternative she had hinted at was even worse.

He sat up straighter, focusing on what remained. Entertainment. The word itself carried weight, unspoken meaning that stretched far beyond the superficial. He had seen enough in his time to understand that power did not vanish, it transformed. And if they were categorizing men like him for "entertainment," it meant some vestige of their influence remained, even if it was twisted beyond recognition.

He forced his voice to remain steady. "You're not executing all of us, then."

Severin's expression remained unchanged. "No. Some of you will serve a different function."

A muscle ticked in his jaw. He had spent his career wielding power like a weapon, knowing that wealth, charm, and leverage could turn any situation in his favor. That instinct didn't disappear overnight. If he could carve out a space where influence still existed, even in some grotesque version of what it had once been, then he could survive this. He could find a way back.

She studied him, her eyes sharp, assessing. "You're thinking of how to manipulate this."

He met her gaze evenly. "You can't erase men like me entirely."

For the first time, the faintest hint of a smirk flickered at the corner of her mouth. "No, we can't. Not yet." She leaned back slightly, tapping a command into the tablet. "But that doesn't mean you'll recognize what you become."

The weight of her words settled in his chest, and for the first time since waking up to this new world, the stark reality of his situation fully formed. There was no return to what he had known. No reclamation of his past life. Even if he survived, even if he maneuvered through this system the way he had maneuvered through every other system before it, the version of himself that existed yesterday was already gone.

A door opened somewhere behind him. The sound of footsteps approached, controlled and deliberate. Severin looked up briefly, then back to him. "Your classification will be finalized shortly," she said. "Until then, you'll be held in temporary processing."

He didn't move at first, his body unwilling to obey an order given so plainly, so unquestionably. He had spent his life issuing commands, never receiving them. But the guards at his back didn't hesitate. A hand closed around his arm, firm, impersonal, and he knew then that whatever autonomy he had left was a phantom, slipping through his fingers like sand.

Severin watched him as he stood. "You should prepare yourself, John-1688A7-ICK2F ," she said, her voice cool, indifferent. "You won't recognize yourself by the time we're done."

Dorian didn't respond. There was nothing left to say. He walked forward, past the woman who had rewritten his fate, past the doors of the chamber where his legacy had ended. He walked, step by step, into the unknown.

Dorian was led down a series of corridors that seemed designed to strip him of any lingering illusion that he was still a man of status. The once-grand civic building had been gutted of its previous grandeur, its interiors reduced to a stark, utilitarian functionality. The echoes of his footsteps, accompanied by those of his silent escorts, bounced off the stone walls, amplifying the void of purpose that had settled deep in his chest. There was no one else in the hallways, no familiar faces, no remnants of the world he had once controlled. It was as if the past had already been erased, and he was merely a ghost passing through it, waiting to be rewritten.

They reached a steel door at the end of a dimly lit hallway. One of the guards pressed a hand against a biometric scanner, and the lock disengaged with a mechanical hiss. The door swung open, revealing a space unlike anything Dorian had anticipated. It wasn't a prison cell, nor was it a courtroom or a chamber for interrogation. Instead, the room resembled something in between, a sterile, clinical environment with a row of chairs lined against the far wall, each one bolted to the floor. In the center of the space, a workstation glowed with the cool blue light of an interactive display. Several women in medical uniforms moved efficiently between stations, their expressions unreadable as they carried out tasks with the kind of precision that suggested this process had been refined to perfection.

Dorian was directed toward one of the chairs, his hesitation met with an unwavering grip on his arm. He clenched his jaw but didn't resist. He knew that resistance would achieve nothing now. He had no leverage, no cards left to play. He lowered himself into the seat, the cold metal pressing against his back, his body stiff with the quiet tension of a man trying to absorb the reality of his situation without allowing it to break him.

One of the women approached, holding a device that resembled a scanner. Without speaking, she lifted it to his temple, and a soft beep registered in the quiet room. She tapped something onto the screen in front of her, then turned toward one of the others. "Final classification confirmed," she said, her voice void of inflection. "Entertainment."

A wave of something dark and sickening rolled through Dorian's gut. Entertainment. It was the only option left to him besides disposal, but the word carried implications that twisted at his insides. It was confirmation that whatever was coming next would strip away the last fragments of his identity, reducing him to something unrecognizable, something meant to serve a function in a world that had already determined he had no inherent worth outside of what they chose to make of him.

One of the other women approached, holding a tablet. "John-1688A7-ICK2F , your status is now official. Your personal history has been erased from all systems. Your biometric access has been reassigned. Any financial holdings, properties, or residual influences you previously maintained have been permanently reallocated to the state. You will no longer be referred to by your former name in any capacity."

Dorian kept his face blank, though the words hit him with the weight of finality. His empire, his legacy, every piece of himself that had once mattered, gone. He had known this was coming, had seen it playing out in front of him since the moment he woke up to a world that no longer recognized his authority. But knowing it and hearing it spoken aloud were two entirely different things. The erasure was complete. He was nothing more than a designation now.

Another woman moved forward, this one holding a medical injector. She pressed it against his neck without warning, and a sharp sting followed before he could react. A cool sensation spread through his veins, numbing, invasive. His vision blurred for a fraction of a second before steadying again. He turned his head slightly, trying to gauge what had just been done to him. The woman answered before he could ask.

"Neurological recalibration," she said plainly. "It will ensure compliance."

His stomach twisted. He knew what that meant. Not mind control, no, that wasn't their style. They didn't need control when they had conditioning. The substance pulsing through his system wasn't designed to erase him, not in the way history had been erased. It was meant to dull him, to soften the sharp edges of who he had been, making him easier to mold. A blank slate for whatever they needed him to become.

He exhaled slowly, letting the reality of it settle. This was not a mistake, not a temporary re-education process. This was permanent. They were making sure of it.

One of the women handed a file to the lead technician. "Assigning him to Sector Red. Placement details to follow."

Sector Red. He didn't know what that meant yet, but he understood the unspoken message behind the words. He was not being stored, not being shelved away in some administrative task. He was being put on display. A relic of the old world, repurposed for the pleasure of the new one.

The technician pressed a command on her screen, and the restraints on the chair released. "Processing is complete," she said, looking at him for the first time. "You'll be transferred shortly."

Dorian stood slowly, the weight of his new reality pressing down on him in full force. He was led toward another door, this one leading out of the processing center. He knew there was no coming back from this. He had entered as Dorian Thorne St. Claire. He was leaving as John-1688A7-ICK2F .

The door slid open, revealing a long hallway bathed in artificial light. He walked forward, his steps steady, even as everything inside him screamed that he was walking into a future where he no longer belonged.

3
The First Executions

Dorian sat in the transport unit, his body tense, hands gripping the edge of the seat as the vehicle hummed forward with calculated precision. The world outside the window moved past in eerie stillness, the streets of Washington, D.C., emptied of their former rulers. He had been here countless times before, stepping out of black sedans with the casual arrogance of a man who owned everything he touched. But today, he was not stepping out onto those marble steps. Today, he was being delivered.

The procession moved through the wide boulevards of the capital, passing once-sacred institutions now gutted and repurposed. The White House still stood, its façade untouched, but it had ceased to be a symbol of power. No guards at the gates. No desperate politicians clinging to their last semblance of control. Congress had been dissolved. The courts had been stripped of their robes and gavels, and the legislative chambers were nothing more than hollowed-out remnants of an order that had been deemed obsolete.

As the vehicle came to a smooth stop, the doors unlocked with a soft hiss. The guards outside waited for no command. They moved with an efficiency that no longer required verbal confirmation. The Rivers had done this before, and they would do it again. Dorian was pulled from the vehicle, his legs stiff from the prolonged ride, and guided toward the towering structure ahead. He recognized the building immediately, the Supreme Court, though its function had changed overnight. Justice was no longer debated within its walls. It was delivered.

Inside, the air was thick with finality. The grand marble columns and sweeping staircases had once carried the weight of laws carefully shaped to protect men like him. Now, those halls carried a different kind of authority. The floors, polished to perfection, reflected a procession of men being led into the central chamber. Some walked in silence, their expressions blank, resigned. Others fought against their captors, the fight in them burning even as it became clear they had already lost. But there were no impassioned speeches, no calls for reason. Those who resisted were subdued quickly, efficiently, without hesitation.

Dorian was directed toward a row of benches at the back of the vast chamber. The seats were already occupied by others, men he knew, men he had once strategized with over bourbon and cigars, their faces drawn tight with varying degrees of comprehension. To his left, a former senator sat rigid, his knuckles white against his lap. To his right, a hedge fund magnate whose empire had collapsed in the early hours of The Flow stared blankly at the front of the room. None of them spoke.

The chamber itself had been redesigned with purpose. The raised bench where justices had once presided had been stripped of its mahogany grandeur, replaced with a sleek, modern platform. In its center stood Dominique Severin. She did not wear robes. She did not need to. The authority in her stance, in her voice, was enough.

"Proceed," she said simply, and the first prisoner was brought forward.

A former Secretary of Defense, his hair once perfectly combed, now disheveled. His suit, tailored for appearances, now wrinkled, hanging off his frame like a costume that no longer fit. His hands were bound, but he held himself with the rigid posture of a man still struggling to believe that this was real. He was forced to his knees before the platform, the echo of his impact against the marble ringing through the chamber.

A woman at the side of the room began reading his charges. The list was long, deliberate, each word spoken with clarity. War crimes. Financial corruption. Crimes against humanity. Dorian had heard these accusations thrown around in political arenas before, but never like this. Never with the weight of certainty behind them. There was no cross-examination, no rebuttal. The evidence had been compiled long before today. The trial was nothing more than a formality, a punctuation mark at the end of a sentence that had already been written.

When the reading concluded, Severin's gaze settled on the man before her. "Do you contest your designation?" she asked, her voice measured.

The former Secretary of Defense swallowed, his Adam's apple bobbing. "This is madness," he rasped, his voice hoarse. "You can't—"

Severin cut him off with a small tilt of her head. "You misunderstand. You are not here to argue. You are here to receive judgment."

The man opened his mouth again, but the sentence had already been delivered.

"Designation: Disposal."

A single word, and it was over.

Dorian watched as the guards moved in without hesitation. The man was pulled to his feet, his protests lost in the echo of the chamber. There was no final plea, no chance for appeal. He was dragged toward the far end of the room, where a secondary door opened into a chamber beyond. Dorian didn't need to see what was inside. The sickening silence that followed was enough.

He forced himself to remain still, to breathe evenly, to keep his expression neutral. This was the new reality. One he had no choice but to accept. And yet, when Severin looked up, her gaze sweeping across the chamber, he felt something cold grip his spine.

She was not finished.

Another name was called. Another man dragged forward. Another designation pronounced. Disposal. Disposal. Disposal.

The executions were swift, efficient. Each man led through the door, none of them returning. The chamber did not reek of blood, did not carry the chaos of panicked bodies. This was not a massacre. This was methodical. A cleansing. A system that had already been built to replace them, now merely carrying out the final steps of transition.

The next name spoken made Dorian's fingers tighten against his thighs.

A name he knew.

A business partner. A man he had once shared stages with, shaking hands in front of cameras, delivering speeches on economic growth while securing backroom deals that kept them both untouchable. A man who had sat beside him in private jets, sipping the finest whiskey, laughing at the idea that they could ever fall.

Now, that man stood before Severin, trembling.

The charges were read. Corruption. Financial devastation. Crimes against society. The words seemed redundant at this point. No one in this room was innocent. The only thing left was the sentence.

Severin didn't ask if he contested it. She only tilted her head slightly before delivering the final word.

"Designation: Disposal."

Dorian's throat tightened as he watched his business partner break. He didn't fight. He didn't argue. He simply fell to his knees, shaking, whispering something Dorian couldn't hear. It didn't matter. The guards pulled him to his feet, carrying him toward the door. He twisted once, looking back at the chamber with wide, unseeing eyes.

Dorian held his gaze for only a second before the door closed behind him.

Severin exhaled softly, as if clearing the air of unnecessary weight. Then she lifted her gaze once more, scanning the room with quiet, unshakable authority.

"Bring in the next."

The executions continued without pause, each name called like a dull drumbeat of inevitability. Dorian sat rigid, forcing himself to remain still as the chamber around him processed its final judgments. He was beginning to understand the depth of The Flow's precision, this was not a chaotic revolution, not a violent purge born out of raw vengeance. It was order. The Rivers had anticipated everything, had mapped out the dismantling of the old world so thoroughly that even now, those awaiting their fate could find no cracks in the system to exploit.

The next name rang out, cutting through the heavy silence. Another man stood, another relic of the past summoned forward. Dorian recognized him instantly. A former media mogul, the kind of man who had shaped narratives with well-placed headlines, who had controlled public perception for decades. Now, he was nothing but a number, standing before Severin, his hands trembling slightly at his sides. The charges were read, deliberate misinformation, inciting violence, using media as a weapon to oppress and deceive. The words echoed through the chamber, and for the first time, Dorian saw something new ripple through the gathered men.

Recognition.

The former titans of industry, the political architects of power, the men who had engineered entire economies, all of them had believed, on some level, that their crimes were too abstract to warrant punishment. They had not pulled triggers or ordered executions. Their sins had been committed behind desks, in conference rooms, in closed-door meetings where the impact of their decisions had been absorbed by those beneath them. But now, it was laid bare. The decisions they had made had not been faceless after all. The reckoning was not theoretical. It was here, in this room, in the trembling hands of a man who had once dictated what the public believed.

Severin did not ask if he contested his designation. She did not need to. The judgment had already been made.

"Designation: Disposal."

The media mogul's knees buckled, and for a moment, Dorian thought he might collapse entirely. Two guards stepped forward, gripping his arms, keeping him upright as they guided him toward the execution chamber. He did not resist. His mouth moved soundlessly, as though he was trying to speak but had lost the ability to form words. Perhaps he had never imagined his own voice being silenced.

Dorian exhaled slowly, keeping his expression blank as the man disappeared beyond the threshold. One by one, the old world was being erased, and he was watching it happen in real time.

A new sound broke the silence. A shift in the chamber's atmosphere, a subtle but unmistakable energy change. The doors at the far end of the room opened, and for the first time since the proceedings had begun, the public was allowed in.

They entered in controlled waves, their movements deliberate. Women of all ages, all backgrounds, filling the chamber with quiet intensity. They did not cheer, did not call for blood. They simply watched, their presence alone a declaration that this was no longer a world built for the comfort of men like Dorian.

The weight of their gazes was suffocating. He had spent his life in control, in spaces where he dictated the terms of engagement, where his voice was the one that mattered. But now, there was no room for him to speak. He was nothing but a relic being catalogued, sorted, and eventually discarded.

Severin turned her attention to the assembled crowd, addressing them for the first time. Her voice was steady, unwavering. "You were told to wait," she said. "To be patient. To endure. And you did." Her gaze swept the room, landing briefly on individuals within the crowd before moving on. "But patience was never meant to be infinite."

A murmur passed through the gathered women, not of dissent, but of something deeper. Agreement. Understanding.

Severin gestured toward the remaining men, the ones still seated, still waiting to hear their names. "These are the architects of your suffering," she continued. "They built the world that stole from you, that caged you, that left you with less and called it fairness." She let the words settle before continuing. "Now, they will know what it means to have no choice."

Dorian's pulse remained steady, but he could feel something shifting in his chest. The words rang true, undeniable. He had seen the statistics, had understood, in a distant and academic way, the imbalance of power. But he had never cared. He had never needed to. Power had shielded him from the consequences of reality. Now, reality had taken power from him entirely.

Another name was called, another man led forward. This time, one of the seated women spoke. Her voice was calm, measured, yet each syllable carried the weight of generations. "Tell us his crimes."

The charges were read, but this time, there was something different in the air. The crowd listened not just as spectators, but as judges. They had been told to wait, to endure. Now, they would bear witness.

When Severin delivered the sentence, the women nodded. No outbursts, no violence, just a shared acknowledgment that justice had finally arrived.

Dorian shifted slightly, his mind turning over the implications of what he was seeing. This was not a moment. This was a movement. One that had been planned for longer than any of them had realized. The men in this room were not merely being punished. They were being replaced.

More executions followed, each one reinforcing the same message. There would be no return to the old world. There would be no negotiations, no settlements, no last-minute reprieves. The Flow had come, and it would not recede.

The final execution of the day was different. The man brought forward had once been a high-ranking judge, one of the architects of the system that had ensured women remained beneath men in every capacity possible. He had ruled on cases that stripped autonomy, that justified violence, that codified oppression into law. His legacy was not one of simple corruption, it was one of destruction.

His sentencing was read with a clarity that echoed through the hall. When Severin looked to the assembled crowd, she did not ask if he contested it. Instead, she asked the women if they agreed.

The response was a single, unified word. "Yes."

Dorian exhaled slowly as the final door closed for the day. The executions would continue tomorrow, and the next day, until there was nothing left of the world that had once existed.

He had always thought that power was absolute. That no matter how much the tides shifted, men like him would always find a way to claw their way back. But as he sat there, surrounded by the ghosts of what had been, he realized he had been wrong.

This was not a revolution.

This was the future.

Dorian remained seated, his hands clasped loosely in his lap, watching as the chamber doors closed once more. The executions had not ended; they had merely been paused for the day. Tomorrow, the process would continue, and the day after that, and the day after that, until every name on their list had been processed. It was a slow, methodical culling of a world that had ruled unchallenged for too long. There was no rush, no riotous fervor, no sense of cruelty for cruelty's sake. This was discipline. This was control.

He shifted slightly, glancing at the screens now illuminating the room. The executions were no longer confined to the chamber. They were being broadcast. Across the city, across the country, across every territory that had once belonged to the old world. The signal had replaced every major network, every station, every social media feed. There was no escape from it.

The camera panned slowly over the chamber, capturing the full weight of what was happening within these walls. The high ceilings, the marble floors, the unshaken faces of the women presiding over judgment. It settled on Severin, who stood at the center of it all, her expression calm, unwavering.

"This is not chaos," she said, her voice carrying through the transmission with quiet authority. "This is not vengeance. This is balance."

The screen shifted, displaying a live feed of another courtroom, one of many now in session. In this one, a former governor stood trembling before his judgment. His crimes were read out in full detail, spanning decades of policy that had eroded rights, siphoned wealth into the hands of the few, denied justice to those who had cried for it. The camera did not shy away from his face as his designation was pronounced.

"Disposal."

A ripple of sound followed, not applause, not celebration. Just acknowledgment. A nation taking stock of what had been done to it and deciding, finally, that enough was enough.

The feed cut to another location, this time a former military general, his uniform stripped of medals, standing before his executioners. The charges were different, war crimes, sanctioned violence, entire communities left to rot under his watch. He stood stiffly as though refusing to bend, but his eyes betrayed the truth. He had never once imagined he would face consequences. And yet, here he was.

Dorian's gaze flickered to the men still seated around him. Some of them had stopped watching, their eyes vacant, staring at the floor as though doing so might somehow make them disappear. Others remained locked on the screen, absorbing every second, every detail. Perhaps they were looking for some sign of leniency, some indication that at least one of them might be spared. But the broadcasts offered no such comfort.

One by one, the trials played out, their outcomes identical in the ways that mattered. The designations varied, some men were sent to labor camps, others to more public humiliations, but for the architects of the past world, there was no alternative. The old world was being wiped clean.

Severin's voice returned to the broadcast. "For too long, power existed without consequence. It dictated without responsibility. That era is over."

Dorian could imagine it now, people sitting in their homes, in cafes, in once-male-dominated boardrooms that no longer belonged to them, watching this new order unfold. There had been so many years of injustice, of imbalance, that he knew, he understood, they were not looking at this as a horror. They were looking at it as something long overdue.

The screen shifted again, this time showing a close-up of a former CEO, a man Dorian had once known well. He had been one of the more careful ones, never leaving a direct trail of blood or scandal behind him, but the evidence had been there, compiled meticulously over the years. Severin did not need to ask if he contested his sentence. She merely glanced at the gathered public, and their answer came in quiet, absolute unison.

"Yes."

The CEO's head fell forward, a breath shuddering from his lips. The guards moved in. The camera did not turn away.

Dorian exhaled, long and slow. He could feel the reality of it creeping into his bones, pressing against him with an inevitability he had never known before. His own trial had not yet come, but it would. And when it did, there would be no appeal, no argument. There would only be judgment.

The broadcast continued, filling the space with its relentless progression. The men in the room shifted, some now unable to mask their fear. One of them, an older man with thinning hair and an air of defeated arrogance, leaned forward, his voice barely above a whisper. "They won't kill us all."

No one answered him.

Dorian knew the truth. They wouldn't need to.

Dorian did not need to ask when his time would come. He knew. He could feel it creeping closer, the weight of it pressing against his ribs like a slow, suffocating force. Around him, the men who remained sat in varying degrees of resignation. Some stared at the floor, hollow and unseeing, their bodies stiff with dread. Others still clenched their fists, eyes flicking toward the doors as though escape were an option. It was not.

The executions had not stopped. The courtroom had become an unceasing engine of judgment, moving through the ranks of the old world with a precision that could only come from years of planning. Every name called, every sentence delivered, every march toward the chamber beyond was a final act in a world that no longer belonged to them. The men of power had spent their lives avoiding consequences, weaving around accountability like it was an inconvenience rather than an inevitability. They had believed themselves untouchable.

Until now.

The broadcast continued, the images displayed on the massive screens shifting seamlessly from one execution to the next. It was no longer only Washington, D.C. The purge had spread, each city carrying out its own reckoning, each tribunal processing the architects of the old world with the same quiet efficiency. Dorian recognized many of the faces that appeared on the screen. Some were men he had worked with, others competitors he had once sought to outmaneuver. They had all stood in the same halls of power, trading favors and securing their own futures at the expense of everyone else. And now, they were falling, one by one.

The air in the chamber shifted. The energy, already heavy with finality, grew sharper, more electric. Dominique Severin had returned to the podium, her presence commanding without effort. She did not need to call for silence. The room adjusted around her naturally, the murmurs dying down as she prepared to speak.

"We are nearing the end of the first phase," she said, her voice even, unhurried. "Many of the names on this list have already received their designations." Her gaze swept over the room, landing briefly on Dorian before moving on. "What remains now are the final deliberations."

Dorian knew what that meant. The highest-ranking figures, the men who had occupied the deepest levels of corruption and control, those trials had been left for last. They were not being processed in the same manner as the others. Their fates had already been decided, but the executions themselves would serve a greater purpose. A lesson. A demonstration of what happened to those who built a world on suffering and believed they would never pay the price.

The chamber doors opened again, and a new figure was brought forward. This time, there was no hesitation, no pretense of a trial. The man was forced to his knees before Severin, his breathing ragged, his eyes darting wildly. He knew what was coming.

"This one needs no introduction," Severin said, addressing the gathered audience. "He was instrumental in the policies that ensured women would never have autonomy over their own bodies. He built his career on the suffering of others and was rewarded for it." She paused, letting the words settle. "Now, he will face the consequences of his own design."

Dorian did not look away as the man was dragged toward the execution chamber. He could still hear his voice, calm, assured, dismissive, justifying his policies in front of cameras, speaking with unwavering confidence as he stripped away freedoms that were never his to take. Now, he was nothing. The door closed behind him, and the silence that followed was absolute.

Another name was called. Another sentence delivered. The end was coming faster now, the space between each judgment narrowing as the last remnants of the old world were swept away. Dorian kept his breathing slow, controlled, refusing to let the tension in his limbs betray him. He had spent his life mastering the art of unreadability. Even now, in the face of his own undoing, he would not give them the satisfaction of fear.

The chamber doors opened again. The name spoken sent a slow, sickening wave of inevitability through his chest.

Dorian Thorne St. Claire.

He stood before he was pulled to his feet, his movements measured, deliberate. He would not be dragged like the others. He would walk. The room did not erupt into murmurs or whispers. His presence at the front of this chamber was not unexpected. His name had been written into this story from the beginning. There was no surprise, no disbelief. This was only another inevitable step in a sequence that had been playing out since the moment The Flow began.

Severin looked at him, her gaze unreadable. She did not read his charges aloud. She did not need to. Everyone in this room, everyone watching, already knew what they were. His crimes were not singular but systemic, woven into the very fabric of the world that had now been unraveled. His wealth, his influence, his power, every bit of it had been built on the suffering of those who now stood in judgment.

She did not ask if he contested his designation. Instead, she simply let the silence stretch between them, giving him the opportunity to speak.

Dorian exhaled, steady. He met her gaze and said nothing.

Severin nodded once, as if he had given the only answer that mattered. "Designation: Entertainment."

The shift in the room was almost imperceptible, but he felt it. A different kind of sentence. Not disposal, not a quick and final end. No, this was something else entirely. Something drawn out. Something meant to be lived.

He was turned away from the podium and led toward the exit, but not toward the chamber that had claimed so many before him.

Instead, he was directed down a separate corridor, one that led not to death, but to something far worse.

As he walked, Dorian let the weight of it settle. He had always known that power did not simply vanish. It was repurposed. Recycled. And now, he would become a part of that system in a way he had never imagined.

The doors ahead of him opened, revealing the path to whatever fate had been decided for him. He did not look back. The corridor stretched ahead, a long and sterile expanse that pulsed with a quiet hum. The walls were seamless, smooth, untouched by time or wear, as if they had been built for permanence. Dorian's steps echoed slightly as he moved forward, the sound swallowed by the vast emptiness surrounding him. He felt the weight of unseen eyes upon him, watching, assessing, waiting to see how he would carry himself now that he had been stripped of choice.

He passed doors on either side, none marked, none offering any clue as to what lay beyond them. The guards flanking him remained silent, their presence more of a reminder than a threat. They did not need to drag him forward. He walked of his own accord, knowing there was no other direction to go.

The final door at the end of the corridor slid open, and for the briefest moment, Dorian allowed himself the indulgence of uncertainty. Then he stepped through, surrendering to the next chapter of his undoing.

4
DTS Tries to Escape

Dorian had never known the feeling of being truly powerless until now. The corridors that led him away from the execution chamber were not those of a condemned man but of something worse, a man who no longer dictated his own fate. He had been sentenced, not to death, but to a slow, deliberate erasure, repurposed into something unrecognizable. And yet, there was still a part of him that refused to accept it.

As he was led down the dim hallway, his mind raced through contingency plans. There had always been an escape hatch, a backdoor, a failsafe for men like him. He had spent decades fortifying his empire with layers of protection, legal, financial, physical. It was unfathomable that all of it could be dismantled overnight. He needed only to get out, to reach the right people, and he could still reclaim control.

The moment his escort loosened their grip as they approached a transfer station, Dorian made his move. A calculated stumble, a shift in balance, his captors' grip faltered just enough. He spun, driving his elbow into the ribs of the guard closest to him. The impact was sharp, precise, enough to force a reflexive release. He didn't hesitate. He sprinted.

The hallway blurred as he pushed forward, every muscle in his body burning with desperation. He had always been a man who moved with certainty, but now, for the first time in his life, he was running not toward something, but away. He reached the end of the corridor and slammed his palm against a biometric panel, praying that some shred of his former identity still held sway. The screen flashed red. Access Denied.

A curse slipped from his lips as he pivoted, scanning for an alternative. He spotted a stairwell. That was his way out. Footsteps thundered behind him, his pursuers were already closing in. He launched himself down the stairs, taking them two at a time, his breath ragged. The building's layout unfolded in his mind like a schematic. There had to be a secondary exit, an unguarded route meant for maintenance crews or service staff. If he could just—

A door burst open ahead of him. Two figures stepped through, blocking his path. One of them, a woman with a cold, knowing expression, merely shook her head.

"You really thought you still had a way out?"

Dorian skidded to a halt, his pulse hammering. He glanced over his shoulder, more guards were descending behind him, cutting off retreat. He was trapped.

The woman took a step forward, tilting her head as she studied him. "You're not the first to try," she said, almost amused. "You won't be the last."

Dorian's jaw clenched. He had never been *one of many*. He had been the architect, the master of the game. Now, he was just another piece being moved across the board, another fallen king awaiting checkmate.

A sharp sting at the base of his neck sent a wave of numbness through his body before his brain even registered what had happened. His legs buckled. The last thing he saw before his vision swam into darkness was the woman's impassive face, watching as he collapsed.

When he woke, he was somewhere else.

The air smelled different, sterile, cold, unfamiliar. His wrists ached; restraints bit into his skin. He was seated, his head lolling forward, a dull fog settling over his thoughts. He tried to lift his arms, to move, but the effort felt sluggish, detached. He blinked hard, willing his vision to sharpen.

A figure stood in front of him, backlit by a harsh overhead light. She was dressed simply, no uniform, no insignia, but there was no mistaking the authority in her stance.

"Dorian Thorne St. Claire," she said, his name rolling off her tongue like a relic of a bygone era.

His throat was dry when he responded. "I don't know what you think this is," he rasped. "But you're making a mistake."

The woman smirked, crossing her arms. "That's where you're wrong," she said. "The mistake was yours. Thinking you could outrun this."

Dorian forced himself to straighten, to summon whatever remnants of his former self remained. "You don't understand. There are people, powerful people, who won't let this happen."

The woman raised an eyebrow, unimpressed. "You mean the people who won't return your calls?"

Dorian's blood ran cold. He had assumed, somewhere deep in his mind, that there was still an ally, still a hand willing to reach down and pull him from the abyss. But the woman's words carried the weight of certainty. He was not just a man in captivity. He was a man who had already been erased.

As if reading his thoughts, she leaned forward slightly. "Your accounts are frozen. Your assets seized. Every offshore account, every hidden fund, you don't own a cent. The moment The Flow began, your entire existence was systematically dismantled." She tilted her head. "And not a single one of your so-called allies lifted a finger."

Dorian exhaled slowly, suppressing the twisting nausea in his gut. He had spent his life building a fortress of influence, ensuring that no one could ever touch him. And yet, the moment the tides shifted, those who had once been eager to stand beside him had vanished without a trace. He was alone.

The woman stepped back, as if allowing him a moment to absorb the weight of it. "You're not here because of what you might still do," she continued. "You're here because of what you've already done."

Dorian's hands curled into fists, the restraints digging into his skin. "And what exactly do you plan to do with me?" he asked, his voice low.

The woman's smirk didn't fade. "That's not for you to decide."

She turned, signaling to someone outside of his line of vision. A moment later, footsteps approached, and a bag was pulled over his head. The world plunged into darkness.

There was no more Dorian Thorne St. Claire.

There was only what they would make of him next.

The darkness beneath the bag was suffocating, but it was the silence that pressed hardest against Dorian's senses. He had been transported before, moved like high-value cargo, but never like this. Never without his say. He counted the seconds, the minutes, but time blurred. The road beneath him was smooth, the vehicle moving at an even pace. Whoever was in control knew what they were doing. There was no rush, no panic. That was worse. Panic meant mistakes. This was precision.

Eventually, the motion stopped. The car doors opened. Hands gripped his arms, firm but not rough, as he was pulled from his seat. The air was different here. Cooler, thinner. Higher altitude? The thought barely formed before he was guided forward, his feet unsteady on ground he couldn't see. A door slid open with a mechanized hum. Another hallway, footsteps echoing. Then a stop. The bag was ripped away.

The sudden exposure of light seared his retinas. He squeezed his eyes shut against the sting, forcing them to adjust. When he finally opened them, the room around him came into focus.

It was clean. Too clean. Sterile walls, seamless metal, no windows. The kind of place designed to give no indication of time or location. A table sat at the center, bolted to the floor, two chairs placed opposite each other. He was not restrained, but that meant nothing. The illusion of freedom was often the most effective form of control.

A single figure stood near the far wall, watching him. A woman. She was not one of the guards, not one of the functionaries that had escorted him here. Her posture was too relaxed, her presence too deliberate. She belonged here in a way he did not. She studied him with an expression that held neither malice nor sympathy. Just curiosity.

"Sit," she said.

Dorian exhaled slowly. He did not obey immediately. A habit. One last vestige of control, however small. But when she merely raised an eyebrow, unfazed by his hesitation, he moved forward and lowered himself into the chair.

The woman took the seat opposite him, setting a tablet down between them. The screen remained dark. She didn't need it yet. This conversation wasn't about information. It was about him.

"You've been unconscious for approximately fourteen hours," she said, matter-of-factly. "You are in a secure facility, off-grid. No access, no communication."

Dorian remained silent. He knew the tactic. Establish dominance, control the flow of information. He had done it himself in negotiations countless times. But this was not a negotiation.

She continued. "Your classification is confirmed. You are now part of the program designated for high-value assets."

He let out a short breath, something resembling a laugh but void of humor. "Assets," he repeated. "That's what I am now?"

She tilted her head slightly. "That's what you always were."

He clenched his jaw but said nothing. He would not give her the satisfaction of reacting.

She leaned forward slightly. "You understand why you weren't disposed of," she said. "Not everyone in your position receives an alternative. You should consider yourself fortunate."

Fortunate. The word coiled in his chest like a living thing, sharp and venomous. He could still hear the doors of the execution chambers closing behind the others, their fates sealed without hesitation. He had not been granted mercy, he had been reassigned.

She tapped the tablet once, and the screen illuminated, displaying a list of names. Some he recognized. Some were already crossed out. "These were your peers," she said. "They are no longer relevant."

He stared at the list, taking in the names that had once commanded industries, governments, movements. They had been titans, just like him. Now, they were nothing but records.

She studied his reaction before continuing. "Your accounts were terminated. Every property, every business, every offshore holding, seized. There is nothing left of your empire."

Dorian inhaled through his nose, steady. He had suspected as much, but hearing it confirmed sent a fresh wave of anger through him. Anger he could not afford to show.

"So," he said, his voice cool, measured. "What happens now?"

She tapped the tablet again, and the list disappeared. In its place, a single document appeared. No title, no identifiers, just one simple line at the top.

John-1688A7-ICK2F : Program Induction.

His skin prickled. The moment stretched, heavy with unspoken implications.

"You will be trained," she said. "You will be conditioned. You will serve."

He leaned back slightly, arching an eyebrow. "And if I refuse?"

Her expression did not change. "Then your designation will be changed to disposal."

The air between them remained still, charged. She did not need to elaborate. There were no appeals. No options. Just one road forward.

Dorian exhaled slowly, a muscle in his jaw twitching. He had spent his entire life calculating probabilities, weighing advantages. There was no advantage here. Only survival.

The woman tapped the tablet again, locking the screen. She stood, straightening her posture. "You'll be taken to processing shortly," she said. "I suggest you accept your circumstances quickly. Resistance will not serve you."

He remained seated as she moved toward the door, his mind working in overdrive. He needed time, needed to understand the depth of his captivity. Needed to find a way to tilt the balance back in his favor.

But when the door closed behind her, leaving him alone in the sterile room, he realized something with unsettling clarity.

For the first time in his life, he had nothing.

No leverage.

No allies.

No escape.

Dorian Thorne St. Claire was gone. Only John-1688A7-ICK2F remained.

Dorian remained seated long after the woman left, staring at the sterile walls around him. The stark, seamless environment offered no clues, no markings, no indication of where he was or how far he had been taken from everything he once controlled. Time had already begun to stretch in unfamiliar ways, and that disturbed him more than anything. There were no windows, no clocks, no sounds from the outside world, only the quiet hum of the ventilation system and the steady pulse of his own breathing. He had lived in control of time, dictated schedules, bent the world to fit his demands. Now, he existed in a vacuum where time meant nothing.

The door slid open, and two figures entered, both dressed in simple but crisp uniforms. Their movements were precise, their expressions devoid of anything resembling personal interest. One carried a tray of what appeared to be food, though the meal was stripped of any luxury he might have once expected. A bland, nutrient-dense square of protein, a small container of water. No silverware. No choices.

"Eat," one of them instructed, placing the tray before him.

Dorian hesitated. He had seen this before. Conditioning did not begin with pain, it began with compliance. Small things, manageable choices, each one a step toward submission. They would not starve him; they would make him choose to eat on their terms. He considered refusing, but he was not yet in a position to resist effectively. He needed to observe, to learn, to measure the space he now occupied.

Slowly, he reached for the food, picking up the protein square and taking a measured bite. It was dry, tasteless, the texture barely resembling anything natural. But he swallowed it down, following it with a sip of water. The figures watched without comment. When he finished, they collected the tray without acknowledgment, as if his compliance had been assumed all along. Then, they stepped back.

The second figure spoke. "Processing will begin now. Stand."

Dorian did not move immediately. He let the words settle, let the moment stretch just enough to assert that he was not fully broken yet. But when he did rise, he did so with deliberate slowness, his body taut with the awareness that every action, every hesitation, was being recorded, measured, analyzed.

They escorted him through a long, empty corridor that smelled faintly of antiseptic. The walls were featureless, the lighting uniform and cold. It was not a prison, at least not in the way he had imagined captivity. There were no chains, no cells, no visible barriers. Yet he could feel the invisible walls closing around him.

They reached a new room, nearly identical to the last, save for the chair positioned in the center. It was not a restraint chair. It was simple, unassuming, upholstered in a muted fabric. Another illusion of choice. He was not being forced to sit, but he would sit nonetheless.

A screen embedded in the opposite wall illuminated. A voice, neutral and measured, filled the space. "Welcome to your orientation. You have been assigned to the Reformation Program, where you will be reconditioned for functional reassignment. Your compliance is expected."

Dorian clenched his jaw, resisting the impulse to scoff. Functional reassignment. He had been branded, stripped of identity, and now he would be reshaped. He had spent his life remaking the world in his image, and now the world was returning the favor.

The screen flickered, displaying a series of images, faces of men he recognized, men who had sat in boardrooms with him, signed deals with him, dined at the same tables. One by one, their faces were marked, their fates listed beneath their names. Labor. Disposal. Entertainment.

The message was clear. There was no appeal. There was no negotiation.

"Your past status is irrelevant. Your history has been erased. What remains is your purpose, and your willingness to serve it."

Dorian's grip on the armrests tightened.

The screen changed again, shifting to what appeared to be footage, an expansive facility, rows of men in uniforms, moving in controlled sequences. Some worked in silence, handling machinery, performing menial labor. Others were on display, dressed and groomed for a different kind of service, their expressions carefully schooled into compliance. None of them spoke.

Dorian forced his breathing to remain steady. This was not a moment for outrage, for defiance. He needed to understand what was coming.

The voice continued. "Your designation as Entertainment requires specialized conditioning. Your training will ensure adaptability, obedience, and aesthetic compliance. You will not be harmed unless your resistance necessitates correction."

His stomach twisted. This was worse than disposal. This was an existence stripped of will, of autonomy, where survival was permitted but never chosen. And yet, he understood the strategy. The most dangerous men were not those who resisted outright. It was those who learned how to work within the system, those who adapted and endured until an opportunity for power presented itself again. He had been one of them.

He needed time. He needed to understand the gaps, the weaknesses, the unspoken rules beneath the surface of this carefully constructed reality.

"Do you have any questions?" the voice asked.

Dorian inhaled slowly. His mind supplied a thousand, but none that would serve him here. Instead, he responded with the only answer that mattered.

"No."

The screen went dark. The figures who had escorted him in did not react, did not offer him any further explanation. They simply gestured for him to stand.

His training would begin now.

As he was led from the room, Dorian allowed himself one final thought. The old world was gone. His name was gone. But he was still here. And that meant, no matter what they did, the game was not over yet.

Dorian was led from the orientation chamber through another unmarked corridor, the silence pressing against him like a weight. He was no longer surprised by the sterility of his surroundings, the sheer lack of identifying markers. This place, wherever it was, had been designed for one purpose: to strip men like him of any remaining sense of identity. The absence of time, of sound beyond the rhythmic hum of ventilation, ensured that every step he took was one closer to dissolution.

His handlers remained impassive, neither cruel nor kind, simply existing as part of the machine that had absorbed him. They did not issue threats. They did not need to. He had already seen what awaited those who resisted. This was not about punishment; it was about restructuring. He had been a ruler, a man who built empires, shaped economies, dictated narratives. Now, he was being reconstructed into something else entirely.

They brought him to a room that was larger than the one before. The walls here were a softer shade of gray, as though someone had decided a hint of warmth might make the transition easier. A single chair sat in the center, this one cushioned, less clinical than the one in the previous chamber. The lighting was less harsh, designed for long-term endurance rather than interrogation. It was another tactic, he knew. A place to make him feel as though he still had control over something, however minuscule.

A woman entered, different from the others who had escorted him. She was older, perhaps in her late forties, her presence entirely devoid of aggression. If anything, she radiated an unsettling patience. She took a seat across from him, crossing her legs with the ease of someone who had done this before, countless times. A tablet rested on the table between them, though she didn't glance at it. She was studying him instead.

"John-1688A7-ICK2F ," she said, not as an address but as a confirmation. "You understand where you are now."

Dorian didn't respond immediately. He met her gaze, searching for an opening, a weakness in the way she carried herself. But there was nothing. She was unshaken. This was not a power struggle, at least, not one he was winning.

"I understand that my previous life is over," he finally said. The words were careful, measured.

She nodded slightly, as if pleased by his willingness to acknowledge reality. "Good," she said. "That means we can begin the real work."

She tapped the tablet once, and the screen came to life. Rows of text, data, projections. "Your classification requires you to undergo several phases of reconditioning," she said. "This process is designed to ensure maximum adaptability. Resistance is expected but ultimately irrelevant."

He leaned back slightly. "And if I don't comply?"

Her lips curved, but it wasn't a smile, it was amusement, barely concealed. "You misunderstand. You are already complying."

He inhaled slowly through his nose, willing his expression to remain neutral. She was right, of course. He had eaten the food. He had followed their instructions. He had entered this room of his own accord, even knowing that there were no alternatives. Compliance wasn't a choice; it was an inevitability.

She studied him for a moment before speaking again. "Your training will begin in incremental phases. First, we assess your psychological resilience. Your ability to adapt."

She gestured to the tablet, pulling up a new screen. A video began to play, grainy, deliberately low-resolution. It showed a man, seated much like he was now, but further along in the process. The man was speaking, but his words were calm, practiced. Not forced, but deliberate.

Dorian frowned, watching. The man was someone he recognized, a former tech mogul, someone who had spoken with the same bravado

Dorian once had. But now, his voice was softer, his posture more relaxed. There was no tension in his shoulders, no fire behind his eyes. He was explaining, in measured tones, how he had come to accept his new reality. How he had *chosen* to embrace it.

Dorian glanced at the woman across from him. "This is meant to convince me?"

She tilted her head slightly. "It's meant to show you what is possible."

The video continued, and Dorian saw subtle cues, the inflection of the voice, the pauses in speech, the way the man's hands moved when he spoke. He wasn't broken. He wasn't drugged or coerced. He had been reshaped, willingly or otherwise, into something new.

The video ended, and the screen went dark. The silence between them stretched.

"You think this will happen to me?" Dorian finally asked.

The woman didn't answer immediately. She stood, smoothing down the fabric of her uniform. "I think," she said, "that the question is not if, but when."

She moved to the door, pausing before she stepped through. "Processing continues tomorrow. Rest while you can."

The door closed behind her, leaving him alone once more.

Dorian sat in silence, his fingers tightening against the armrests. He had spent his life believing he could shape any narrative, control any outcome. But for the first time, the story was being written around him, and he had no pen in his hand.

He exhaled slowly, staring at the darkened screen where the other man had spoken. He could see his own reflection faintly in the black glass, but for how much longer? How long before the image looking back at him would be someone else entirely?

The room around him felt smaller now, its stark walls pressing inward, as if the very air had thickened. He forced himself to sit still, to resist the restless energy curling in his limbs. He had always been the one orchestrating the performance, pulling the strings. Now, he was on the other side of the glass, an audience to his own unraveling.

The silence hummed with weight, broken only by the distant hum of the facility beyond his door. There was no escape, no backchannel negotiation to be made. The power he had once wielded had been stripped, and in its place, an unfamiliar vulnerability settled in.

For the first time, he truly understood the meaning of inevitability. It was not an abrupt descent but a slow erosion, each moment chipping away at the foundation of what he once was. Tomorrow, the next layer would be removed. And the day after that, another. Until there was nothing left of Dorian Thorne St. Claire at all.

5
The Digital Memory Hole

Dorian sat in the stark confines of his new reality, the walls around him neither closing in nor offering comfort. Time had begun to lose meaning. The concept of morning and night no longer applied when the artificial lighting overhead remained the same, indifferent to the rhythm of the world beyond. He knew things were happening outside these walls. He could feel the shift, the slow but deliberate dismantling of what once was. The power he had wielded, the empire he had built, the legacy he had constructed over decades, it was all being unmade in real time, and he was powerless to stop it.

A screen embedded into the wall flickered to life, unprompted. He had stopped reacting to these sudden intrusions days ago. The screen, like everything else in this place, operated without his consent, without his input. He was no longer an active participant in his own existence; he was merely a witness to his own erasure.

The first image that appeared was one he recognized instantly, St. Claire's Media's unmistakable skyline, the headquarters that once stood as a monument to his influence. The name was gone. The signage had been replaced. No more St. Claire. No legacy remained attached to the empire he had spent his life building. The camera angle shifted, giving a panoramic view of what had replaced it: a massive screen dominating the side of the building, broadcasting new images, new narratives. Women's faces filled the digital billboards, figures of power and leadership, their names the ones now written into history. He recognized none of them. The voice-over was calm, authoritative, final.

"The revision is complete. The old world is no longer relevant."

Dorian exhaled slowly, feeling a numbness settle in his limbs. He had expected retribution, humiliation, even pain. But this was something else. This was deeper. He was being unmade in real time.

The feed transitioned to footage from across the world, statues being pulled down in grand city squares, marble and bronze shattered against concrete. Not all were destroyed; some were altered. Male faces reshaped, features softened, inscriptions rewritten to honor women who had, until now, existed in the shadows of history. The past was being edited with the same ruthless efficiency as the present.

A historian appeared on the screen, her voice measured as she narrated the changes. "What we called history was nothing more than a record of those in power. We are correcting a mistake, not erasing the truth." Behind her, the monuments to war, conquest, and political dominance crumbled. Some were burned, melted down to repurpose materials into new works. New statues rose in their place. The message was clear: there would be no restoration of the old world.

The screen shifted again. A familiar image appeared, one that sent an unfamiliar heat rising in his throat. His own face. A, moment later, it disappeared.

His name dissolved from search databases, his quotes removed from articles, his contributions wiped from business records. The companies he had founded still existed, but not under his name. They had never been his. The stock tickers continued, the markets still moved, but he no longer held any stake in them. His wealth had not only been seized, it had been forgotten.

For the first time since he had been taken, his pulse spiked. This was not imprisonment. This was erasure.

The video feed continued, moving through layers of society that had once been built on the foundation of men like him. The banking sector, once dominated by old money, had been restructured to serve an entirely different economic model. The names of once-powerful financiers were gone, replaced by new leadership. Historic treaties, legislation, court rulings, rewritten, their authorship attributed elsewhere. Military victories that had shaped the world stage no longer bore the names of the men who had orchestrated them. Wars that had been waged, justifications that had been given, entire narratives of conquest and expansion, altered to reflect a different reality.

He had expected them to come for the future, to take control of what lay ahead. But they were doing something far more dangerous. They were unraveling the past. Not only had he been removed from power, he had been removed from memory itself.

He turned away from the screen, squeezing his eyes shut. He had spent years cultivating an image, a brand that extended beyond wealth, beyond business. He had made himself into something indelible, a force that could not be ignored, a man whose name carried weight in every room he entered. Now, he was watching that weight dissolve, grain by grain, slipping through the cracks of the very system he had once used to ensure his permanence.

The screen transitioned again, this time showing the mass deletions from digital archives. Libraries, universities, institutions that had once stored vast amounts of historical documentation—now stripped of his presence. His books, his articles, the interviews he had given over decades, vanished. No citations, no attributions. The journalists who had once quoted him now referenced different sources, as if he had never spoken at all. It was as though the last twenty years of his life had been rewritten in a single keystroke.

The voice returned, impersonal, unbothered by the destruction it described. "The records are complete. The past has been corrected."

Dorian's hands clenched into fists at his sides. He knew, logically, that resistance was meaningless. That no one was coming for him, that no plea or argument would restore what had been taken. But the truth of it burned in his veins. This was not just punishment. This was the undoing of everything he had been.

And then the final image filled the screen.

A list of names, long and scrolling, names that had once dominated every sphere of influence, media moguls, financial titans, political strategists, military generals. Every name crossed out. Every achievement reassigned. The words at the top of the list stood out in bold clarity:

Retracted Influence: The Final Correction.

Dorian stared at it, his breath slow, his body still. He had always believed that history could not be rewritten, that power left an imprint too deep to be erased. But the screen in front of him told a different story.

He had not just lost.

He had ceased to exist.

Dorian sat unmoving, his gaze locked on the now-dark screen, the finality of what he had just witnessed settling into his bones like a slow, creeping frost. He had always believed power was an indelible force, that no matter how drastically systems changed, the architects of the past would remain embedded in its foundations. But he was wrong. This was not just a coup, not merely the fall of an empire. It was a systematic forgetting, an unraveling of the very idea that men like him had ever shaped the world.

He leaned back against the cold, unyielding wall, his pulse steady but his thoughts racing. This wasn't just punishment, it was replacement. In the past, revolutions had taken down regimes but left their remnants behind, echoes of their existence that persisted in history books, in whispered conversations, in old footage archived for future analysis. This was something else. There would be no remnants, no whispers. The Flow was rewriting reality itself, ensuring there was nothing left to preserve, no footnotes to hint at what had come before.

The door to his cell slid open without a sound, and a new figure entered. A woman, sharply dressed, her presence carrying the weight of quiet authority. She did not rush. She did not posture. She was not here to threaten him. She didn't need to. The power imbalance had already been established, and he was on the wrong end of it.

“You’ve seen it now,” she said simply, stepping toward the chair opposite him and lowering herself into it. She regarded him with an expression that was not gloating, not cruel, but merely observational, as if he were an equation she was watching unfold.

Dorian inhaled slowly, considering his words before speaking. “What happens next?”

She tilted her head slightly, studying him. “That depends on you.”

He let out a quiet, humorless chuckle. “You say that like I have a choice.”

She gave a small nod. “Not in the way you think. You no longer exist, Dorian Thorne St. Claire. But that doesn’t mean you can’t be useful.”

He clenched his jaw. That word again, *useful.* He had spent his entire life ensuring his utility, his indispensability. It had been the foundation of his power, the reason he had remained untouchable for so long. And now, even in captivity, they dangled that same promise in front of him, as if survival depended on proving his worth all over again.

She gestured toward the screen, which flickered back to life. This time, it displayed an array of articles, documents, headlines, publications that had once featured his name. Only now, each one had been revised, his contributions reassigned to others, his image replaced by figures he did not recognize. It was not only his name that had been erased but the very narrative of his achievements.

“You see, the world doesn’t need men like you anymore,” she continued, her voice even. “What you built will remain, but the story has changed. Your influence was never essential, it was circumstantial. Now, that circumstance has changed.”

Dorian’s eyes lingered on a headline about an economic summit he had once dominated, his policies shaping markets for decades. The article was still there, but he was not. Another name had taken his place. His thoughts churned, the sheer scale of what had been done gnawing at the edges of his resolve. This was not merely the fall of a man. This was the cleansing of an entire lineage of power.

The woman leaned forward slightly, her hands folding on the table between them. “You’re struggling with the idea that you were never as permanent as you believed. That the world doesn’t crumble without you. That it, in fact, moves on quite efficiently.”

His silence was answer enough.

She exhaled through her nose, almost sympathetically. “History isn’t as rigid as you thought, Mr. St. Claire. It’s malleable. People accept what they are given, as long as it is structured well enough. And The Flow has ensured that this transition is seamless.”

He wanted to argue, to insist that people would notice, that the world could not simply forget so many of its former rulers, but the evidence was already in front of him. They weren’t just erasing, they were replacing. The system had been redesigned in such a way that people were already accepting the new reality. Without hesitation. Without question.

“What do you want from me?” he finally asked, his voice quieter than before.

She studied him for a moment longer before tapping the screen. The display changed again, showing lists of men, names that had once carried the same weight as his. Some were marked for disposal. Others had been reassigned. But a select few had been categorized under a different designation: *Reformation.*

“You are at a crossroads,” she said. “There are only two paths left for men like you. One leads to complete disposal. The other leads to integration.”

Dorian’s jaw tightened. “Integration into what?”

Her lips curved, but not into a smile. It was something colder, more precise. “Into the world that replaces the one you built.”

He exhaled slowly, looking back at the names on the screen. Some he had worked with. Some he had competed against. Some he had personally crushed under the weight of his own ambitions. Now, they were nothing more than remnants of a system that had already been discarded. And he was on the precipice of joining them.

The woman stood, smoothing the fabric of her jacket as she stepped back toward the door. "We will give you time," she said. "Not much. But enough to decide how you want to exist in what comes next."

The door opened, and she disappeared into the corridor beyond, leaving him alone once more.

Dorian sat in silence, the weight of his own nonexistence pressing down on him. He had built a world where power was the only currency that mattered. Now, he existed in one where he was broke.

And for the first time in his life, he didn't know how to buy his way out.

Dorian sat in the silence left behind by the woman's departure, his mind grinding through the implications of what he had just been told. Integration. The word itself felt clinical, neutral, but he knew better. There was no neutrality in what had been done to him, in what was still being done to the remnants of his world. The system had no interest in allowing him to return to even a fraction of what he had once been. The terms of survival were clear: obedience or oblivion.

He forced himself to breathe evenly, his fingers pressing into his knees as he weighed his nonexistent options. For the first time in his life, he had no leverage, no assets to maneuver. He had spent years believing that power was about positioning, about knowing which hand to play at the right time. But there were no hands left to play. They had taken everything. More than his wealth, more than his title. They had stripped him of identity itself.

The screen flickered on again, but this time, it did not show him erasures or rewritten headlines. Instead, it displayed a controlled feed of the world outside, a world where he had never existed. The cityscapes were the same, the skyscrapers and financial districts still bustling with activity. But the faces running the world were different. The halls of power were occupied by new figures, women whose authority had been seamlessly woven into the narrative of history, as though they had always been there. It was not just replacement. It was as if his kind had never ruled at all.

He leaned forward, studying the movements of the world he had once commanded. News panels discussed policy shifts, economic strategies, foreign diplomacy. The changes were subtle but undeniable. The hunger for dominance, for conquest, was absent. There was no language of exponential growth, no demands for aggressive market expansion or resource exploitation. It was a world of calculated sustainability, of equity-driven decisions. A world no longer engineered for men like him.

The door slid open once more, and a new figure entered. This one was younger than the woman before, her expression devoid of the quiet amusement the last had carried. She did not sit. She stood near the door, watching him with something closer to indifference. The same way he had once looked at people he knew had no future.

"You've had time," she said flatly. "What's your decision?"

Dorian let his lips part slightly, as if about to respond, but no words came. He didn't know what answer would even matter. What did integration mean? Would he be placed in a role, assigned a function? Would he still be himself in any meaningful way, or would the process strip him of even that?

She tilted her head slightly, watching his hesitation with the patience of someone who already knew the outcome. "Let me clarify something for you," she said. "Integration is not an offer. It is a transition. You do not negotiate. You adjust."

His hands tightened into fists. "And if I refuse?"

For the first time, her expression shifted, a flicker of something close to curiosity crossing her face. "Then you join the others in disposal."

He exhaled slowly, a humorless chuckle leaving his lips. "So I either become something useful to you or I disappear."

She nodded. "Yes."

Dorian leaned back, considering her, considering everything. He could refuse. Let them wipe him from the last remaining places where he might still exist. Let them reduce him to nothingness, let his story end in total erasure. But something in him resisted. Some deep, burning part of him refused to let them dictate the final note of his existence.

The woman took his silence as consent, stepping forward and placing a thin device on the table before him. A tablet, but unlike any he had seen before. The screen activated the moment it registered his presence, and a file opened with his new designation: Reformed Asset –John-1688A7-ICK2F.

His throat tightened at the sight of the name. Not Dorian. Not St. Claire. Just a numbered unit in their new world.

"Your program begins immediately," she said, gesturing toward the screen. "You will be trained in the necessary skills required for your reassignment. Resistance will only extend the process. And I assure you, that is not in your best interest."

He scanned the file. Training. Compliance testing. Psychological reconditioning. Every step of his integration was outlined with brutal efficiency. There was no appeal. This was not a negotiation. It was an assimilation.

His fingers hovered over the confirmation tab on the screen. One press, and he accepted whatever version of himself they had carved out. One press, and he continued to exist, just not as the man he had once been.

He looked up at the woman, meeting her gaze one last time before making his choice.

Dorian's fingers hovered over the confirmation tab, his mind running through every possible outcome. There was no winning here. He had lost everything already, his wealth, his influence, his past. The only thing left was survival, but even that wasn't truly survival, was it? Survival implied maintaining some shred of the self, of the man he had once been. But this wasn't about survival. It was about submission.

The woman across from him remained silent, waiting with the patience of someone who had witnessed this moment hundreds of times before. She didn't need to convince him. The weight of inevitability did that for her. There was nowhere to run. No resources to leverage. No allies left to call. The old world was gone, and his presence in it had been erased as if he had never existed at all.

His thumb pressed the screen.

A quiet chime confirmed his acceptance. The woman did not react, no note of victory or satisfaction. Just a simple nod, as though he had only done what was expected. She retrieved the tablet, tapping a few commands before placing it back into her pocket. "You'll begin immediately," she said. "Stand."

Dorian swallowed the bitterness rising in his throat. He did as instructed. If he was going to get through this, he needed to observe, to learn the rules of the new system. He would not resist outright. Not yet. That wasn't how survival worked. He had built an empire off of reading the tides of power, of knowing when to push and when to let the current carry him. That instinct had not left him, even now.

The woman led him through the door, the hallway beyond identical to every other sterile corridor he had seen since his capture. No windows, no markings, nothing to give him any sense of direction. It was a structure designed for disorientation, stripping him of any ability to gauge his location or map an escape.

After several turns, they reached a door that slid open with a mechanical hiss, revealing a vast space beyond. The room was expansive, lined with glass partitions that separated it into different stations. Some held men like him, seated before monitors, their eyes locked on training materials as streams of text rolled past their screens. Others stood in controlled formations, reciting lines in unison, their voices low and rhythmic. A few, further down, were being fitted into new clothing, their final uniforms, their last identity.

Dorian took in every detail. The men did not look broken, not in the traditional sense. They were not shackled, not visibly restrained. And yet, none of them deviated from their assigned tasks. None of them spoke outside of instruction. It was a different kind of control, one that had bypassed brute force and gone straight to the mind.

The woman turned to him. "Your processing begins here."

Two figures approached, both women, both dressed in the same neutral uniforms. One held a tablet, the other a measuring instrument of some kind. They flanked him without hesitation, one beginning to scan his body dimensions while the other pulled up his newly assigned profile.

"John-1688A7-ICK2F ," the first woman said, reading from the tablet. "Designated for Reformation Program, Tier Three."

Dorian stiffened slightly at the sound of the name. His name. But it wasn't his name. It was the label they had given him, a numerical designation that severed him from everything he had once been. He forced himself to remain still, offering no outward reaction.

The second woman finished her scan and nodded to the first. "He'll need full cognitive recalibration before his first assignment."

Dorian's pulse ticked up slightly. Recalibration. He knew what that meant. Not just training, not just instruction, but rewiring. A forced reshaping of thought, of response. They didn't just want compliance. They wanted belief.

He took a slow breath, nodding once as though acknowledging an order. He had no intention of allowing them to break him, but he needed to see their methods firsthand. He needed to understand what was happening to the others if he had any hope of resisting in the future.

The first woman gestured toward one of the empty stations. "Sit. Begin."

Dorian moved without argument, taking his place before the screen. As soon as he settled, the interface came to life, a series of images flashing before his eyes, paired with text, audio, and structured questions. He recognized the technique immediately. Conditioning. Exposure training. It was designed to overwrite old associations, to introduce new ways of processing information until the mind naturally accepted them as truth.

The first module displayed a historical event, one he knew well. One he had lived through. But the names were different. The details altered. Where he had once been a player in the outcome, he was absent. Someone else stood in his place, taking credit for decisions he had made, for victories he had orchestrated. The screen prompted a response.

Who was responsible for the success of the 2008 economic recovery?

The options were all women. His name was not there. Not even as a forgotten footnote.

His fingers hesitated over the input device. He knew what they wanted. He knew what the correct answer was in this new world.

He selected it.

The screen moved forward without hesitation. Good. Progress recorded.

Dorian let out a slow breath. He had chosen correctly, but the tightness in his chest remained. How long before every memory, every fact, every fundamental truth he knew was rewritten? How long before he started questioning what was real and what had only been real to him?

Another module. Another question. Who were the architects of the new world?

Again, only one kind of answer was acceptable.

And so it went, question after question, module after module. He progressed through hours of material, his body rigid, his mind fighting against the slow creep of acceptance. He knew how these systems worked. Repetition. Reinforcement. Reward for compliance. Correction for deviation.

As the modules continued, a strange, numbing sensation settled in. The repetition was hypnotic, each correction chipping away at what he thought he knew. He wondered how long it would take for it to feel normal, how long before he stopped thinking about what was missing and simply accepted what was given. That was their true method, not destruction, but redirection. Not pain, but fatigue. A slow, inevitable erosion of resistance.

By the time the session ended, his thoughts were sluggish, the weight of the hours spent in compliance pressing against him. The message on the screen confirmed his standing.

Progress: Acceptable. Additional conditioning scheduled.

Dorian exhaled, feeling the tension in his shoulders for the first time. The session was over. For now.

The woman who had led him here returned, glancing at the monitor before meeting his gaze. "You've begun well," she said. "Continue adapting, and the transition will be painless."

Dorian stood, his body stiff but his expression carefully controlled. He had adapted. He had survived. But the question remained: for how long?

As he was led away from the station, he forced himself to replay the information, to commit it to memory in its unaltered form. He had lost control over what was recorded, but not over what he chose to remember. That was the only battle he could still fight. The one in his own mind.

Dorian forced himself to keep his breathing steady as he was escorted from the training chamber, his mind still vibrating from the sheer intensity of the session. His fingers twitched slightly, the muscle memory of selecting the 'correct' answers still lingering. He had passed their test, for now. But the weight of what lay ahead pressed against him like an iron band around his chest. This was only the beginning.

The corridors blurred past as they led him forward, deeper into the facility. Another door, another room. This one was smaller, more personal, lined with simple chairs and a single table. He was guided to a seat, and for the first time since his processing began, another man was brought into the room with him.

The man was older, perhaps in his fifties, with graying hair and the sharp, sunken eyes of someone who had once commanded power but had long since been broken by its absence. He looked at Dorian, recognition flickering in his gaze. They had known each other, once. Sat at the same tables, dictated the same markets. Now, they were nothing.

The woman overseeing them tapped her screen. "You will assist in each other's transition. Conversation is permitted, but deviation is not."

6
The New Order Speaks

Dorian sat in the stark confines of what had once been an observation room, now repurposed for those like him, assets, men who had been stripped of autonomy, reduced to spectators of a world they no longer belonged to. The screen embedded in the wall flickered to life, the broadcast beginning without preamble, without a flourish of introductions or dramatics. This was not a spectacle for the people. This was an announcement for the world.

Carmilla Kahlo's image filled the screen, her presence commanding yet unnervingly calm. She did not raise her voice. She did not need to. Authority was woven into her every movement, her every carefully measured pause. Behind her, the insignia of TIDE loomed, the emblem now universally recognized as the force that had overturned centuries of male dominion.

Her gaze was direct, unwavering. She did not speak in the careful, rehearsed rhetoric of old-world politicians, the ones who had cloaked cruelty in diplomacy. There was no appeal for understanding, no attempts to justify what had been done. She simply spoke.

"This is not a negotiation."

The words cut through the silence like a blade. Dorian felt them settle in his chest, a final, irrevocable truth.

"You did not negotiate with us when you ruled. You did not ask for permission to structure the world to your liking, to hoard power while calling it merit, to break the backs of those who served you and tell them it was their duty. You built nations on the idea that your control was natural. Now, we take what was never yours to begin with."

She did not raise her voice, yet it reverberated in the bones of every man forced to listen.

Dorian's hands curled into fists at his sides. It wasn't the words that unsettled him, it was the certainty behind them. This was not the start of a debate. This was the declaration of the future, and men like him had no place in it.

The broadcast continued, shifting from Carmilla's direct address to footage from around the world. The restructuring of society was already well underway. What had once been boardrooms filled with suits and whispered deals now held women governing in open assemblies, decisions made not in secret but in transparent policy. Economic systems had been dismantled and restructured, wealth no longer funneled toward the few but redistributed in ways that ensured no one could build an empire of unchecked dominance again. It was a world that no longer rewarded greed, aggression, or calculated ruthlessness, the very traits that had built Dorian's success.

His stomach tightened as the feed shifted again. This time, it was not policy changes or structural reforms. This time, it was about men.

TIDE had classified them. A new order, a new purpose, a clear delineation of their place in the world that had been rewritten.

Labor. The majority had been assigned here, stripped of their former lives and placed into the industries that required the most manpower. Infrastructure, agriculture, sanitation, transportation, physical roles, their contributions reduced to sweat and toil. The footage showed long lines of men, dressed in simple, identical uniforms, working under the guidance of overseers who did not need to bark orders. Compliance had already been conditioned.

Pleasure. The second classification was more selective, the process more meticulous. Those deemed physically desirable, genetically superior in ways that benefited the new society, were assigned to roles where their bodies were their only currency. They were trained, conditioned, and displayed. The footage did not show their final destinations, but it did not need to. The implication was clear.

Disposal. The rest had been deemed unfit for either. They had no purpose in the new world. And so, they were simply removed.

Dorian's breath was slow, measured, but his pulse throbbed at his temples as he watched the final category play out on the screen. The men were led, in orderly lines, into the facilities designated for disposal. There was no spectacle, no dramatic executions. They simply ceased to be.

The screen returned to Carmilla. She let the silence stretch, letting the weight of what had been revealed settle before she spoke again.

"This is not cruelty," she said, as though answering the unspoken arguments of every man who had once believed themselves indispensable. "This is balance."

Dorian closed his eyes for a brief moment, the implications settling over him like an avalanche. He was still here. He had not been disposed of. But that did not mean he had been spared.

Dorian's eyes remained locked on the screen long after the image of Carmilla Kahlo faded into darkness. The words still echoed in his mind, reverberating with an intensity that made it impossible to focus on anything else. This is not cruelty. This is balance. He clenched his fists, feeling the nails bite into his palms. It was a strange sensation, knowing that he still had a body, still occupied space, yet existed as nothing more than a relic of a time that had ceased to be relevant.

The door to his holding cell slid open with its usual mechanical precision, but this time, two figures entered. One was a woman he had not seen before, her uniform crisp, her expression unreadable. The other was a man, younger, barely more than a boy, his posture stiff with barely contained tension. Dorian immediately recognized the difference. The woman carried herself with the authority of someone who knew she was in control. The man, by contrast, carried himself like someone who knew his position was temporary.

"Stand," the woman ordered.

Dorian did as he was told. There was no hesitation. Compliance was not instinctual, but it was necessary. He had spent too long in this place not to understand that much. He had watched other men resist, watched them struggle against what was happening. They were no longer here.

The young man stepped forward, tablet in hand. His hands trembled slightly as he tapped at the screen, pulling up what Dorian knew was his classification assignment. The tension in the room was palpable, but neither figure seemed to acknowledge it. The woman gestured toward the screen. "John-1688A7-ICK2F , your classification has been finalized."

Dorian inhaled slowly, bracing himself.

"You are property."

The words struck with a finality that he had not been prepared for, even after everything he had seen, everything he had endured. Property. A designation lower than labor, lower than pleasure. He was not assigned to build, nor to serve in entertainment. He was an object, something owned, something without rights.

His throat tightened, but he forced his breathing to remain steady. This was not the time to react. This was the time to understand. To absorb.

The woman continued as if she had merely assigned him to a desk job. "You will be processed for reassignment shortly. Your personal history is irrelevant. Your former status is irrelevant. Your previous contributions are irrelevant. From this point forward, you exist solely for the use of those who own you."

She handed the tablet back to the young man, who swallowed hard before continuing. His voice was thinner, less certain. "Your initial transfer will occur within twenty-four hours. You will receive a preliminary assessment to determine suitability for further modification."

Modification. Dorian's pulse quickened, but he remained still. The word was vague, deliberately so, but it implied something beyond simple labor. They were not simply classifying men; they were reshaping them.

"Where am I being transferred?" he asked, his voice even, though he already knew the question was meaningless.

The woman regarded him for a moment, then glanced at the young man. He hesitated before checking the tablet. His throat bobbed. "A Tier-One estate. Private ownership."

Dorian had seen glimpses of what that meant. The private estates were the most exclusive sector of The Flow's restructuring, places where the last remnants of male identity were molded, reshaped, and ultimately erased. No man sent to a Tier-One estate ever resurfaced unchanged.

He exhaled slowly, keeping his expression neutral.

The woman turned toward the door. "You will be escorted shortly. Prepare yourself."

She left without another word, but the young man lingered, hesitating for just a fraction of a second before following. A hesitation that had not gone unnoticed.

Dorian filed that detail away. There were still cracks in the system, however small.

Alone once more, he sat down, staring at the blank screen where Carmilla Kahlo's face had once been. Property. The word repeated in his mind, an immutable verdict. There would be no trial, no appeal. He did not belong to himself anymore.

His breathing slowed, his thoughts settling into something sharper, something colder. The rules had changed. The board had been wiped clean. But the game was still being played.

And he had no intention of losing.

The wait for transport was excruciating, not in its length, but in its absolute lack of information. Hours passed in silence, no sound but the rhythmic hum of the ventilation system. He was left alone in his own mind, replaying every interaction, every word spoken by those who now held his fate in their hands. He thought of the younger man, his hesitation. The flicker of something resembling uncertainty in his expression. Not all of them were fully indoctrinated yet. That was something.

When the door finally opened again, it was not to inform him of anything, nor to provide an update. Instead, a small team entered, their movements rehearsed, efficient. No words were spoken as they pulled him to his feet, securing a band around his wrist, a tracker, he assumed. They did not chain him. They did not need to. There was nowhere to go, no exits unguarded, no passage unmonitored.

They led him through a series of hallways, each identical to the last, until they reached a transport bay. Several other men stood in formation, heads bowed, eyes unseeing. Their clothing was the same, standardized gray garments that stripped them of individuality. Dorian joined them, falling into line without instruction.

A voice spoke from somewhere ahead. "Board."

One by one, the men stepped forward, entering the transport vehicle, an unmarked shuttle with darkened windows. When it was Dorian's turn, he hesitated for only a fraction of a second, inhaling sharply before stepping inside. He took his seat as the doors sealed behind them, locking them into silence once more.

The shuttle hummed to life, lifting off with a smoothness that suggested advanced technology, a precision-engineered transition to another stage of their new reality. Dorian watched the other men, their faces impassive, their expressions hollow. Some had already lost the fight within themselves. Some had accepted what they had become.

Dorian had not.

As the shuttle carried them toward their final destination, he made a silent promise to himself. He might be property now. But that did not mean he would remain so forever.

The shuttle moved with a precision-engineered silence, the kind that suggested it was designed for efficiency rather than comfort. Dorian sat rigidly in his seat, the hum of the engines beneath him a distant vibration he barely registered. The men around him, his fellow captives, remained in their assigned positions, unresponsive to the passage of time. Some were already lost, their gazes empty, their bodies slouched in quiet resignation. Others remained outwardly composed but carried a rigid tension in their postures. They understood the weight of what was coming, even if they didn't yet know the details.

Dorian forced himself to remain analytical. Emotion had no place here. Fear, anger, desperation, none of it would serve him. He needed to observe. He needed to absorb every detail, every movement, every unspoken rule that governed this system. The more he understood, the better chance he had of navigating it.

After what felt like hours, the shuttle began its descent. There were no windows, but the subtle shift in pressure, the change in gravity, signaled their arrival. The moment the engines powered down, the doors hissed open, revealing a stark, industrialized landing bay. Bright white lights flooded the interior, casting sharp, sterile shadows against the steel walls. No sound accompanied the opening, no commands, no orders. The process was automated, seamless. The absence of direct instruction was another form of control. They were expected to know what to do.

The men stood in unison. Dorian followed, stepping onto the landing platform. The facility stretched outward in clean, calculated lines, a fortress of cold efficiency. Towering walls enclosed the compound, punctuated by reinforced gates and sentry stations. The entire structure hummed with power, a quiet, omnipresent reminder of its authority.

They were ushered forward by silent enforcers, women clad in uniforms without insignia, their presence commanding without the need for visible weapons. Dorian noted the way they moved, fluid, assured, without hesitation. They did not fear the men in their charge. They did not need to.

A secondary transport awaited them, a series of enclosed tram-like vehicles lined up along a rail system. The group was separated, split into smaller units, each directed toward a different vehicle. Dorian was pushed toward one of the middle compartments, stepping inside as the doors sealed behind him.

Inside, the space was minimal, seating along the walls, a central control panel embedded into the ceiling, no visible controls or windows. The journey resumed. He could feel the movement beneath him, but there was no indication of their speed or direction.

Minutes passed. Then the tram slowed. Another automated hiss, another door sliding open. This time, the environment was different. The sterility of the landing bay had given way to something more controlled, more curated. The architecture was smoother, almost elegant in its design. The Tier-One estate.

Dorian stepped out into a structured courtyard, surrounded by towering stone walls and open sky. The air smelled different, clean, curated, almost artificial in its perfection. This was not a prison, not in the traditional sense. This was something more insidious. A place designed not to punish, but to reshape.

A woman waited at the entrance, flanked by two attendants. Unlike the uniformed enforcers, she wore something more refined, a tailored suit, high-collared, precise. Her presence radiated an effortless authority, the kind that came from absolute control over one's surroundings.

She studied the arrivals for a moment before speaking. "Welcome to your new designation," she said simply, her voice smooth, clinical.

"You are no longer classified as individuals. You are assets. You will refer to yourselves accordingly."

Dorian said nothing. He had no intention of speaking unless absolutely necessary.

The woman continued, her gaze sweeping over them like a surveyor inspecting newly acquired property. "Your integration begins immediately. You will undergo reassignment based on suitability. Your previous identity holds no relevance. Your function will be determined by your capacity to adapt."

She gestured, and the attendants stepped forward, dividing them into smaller groups. Dorian was pulled into a line with five others, guided toward an interior corridor.

The walls here were smooth, neutral in color, designed for efficiency rather than comfort. They passed through a series of checkpoints, their movements tracked, their presence noted but never acknowledged directly. They were already part of the system.

At the final checkpoint, the group was directed toward an individual processing station. Each man was assigned to a chamber, a featureless, enclosed room containing nothing but a single chair and a display screen. Dorian sat as instructed, his back straight, his expression unreadable. The screen flickered to life, displaying a new directive:

Acknowledgment of Status:

A list of conditions followed, each statement reinforcing what had already been said, identity erased, classification reassigned, compliance mandatory. A single prompt appeared at the bottom of the screen: Confirm Understanding.

Dorian stared at it. The choice was an illusion. There was only one option.

He pressed the confirmation tab.

The display shifted. New text appeared, detailing the next phase of integration.

Stage One: Adaptation

"You will undergo conditioning designed to accelerate your transition. Compliance will be rewarded. Resistance will not be tolerated."

Dorian inhaled slowly. This was not the end. It was only the beginning.

Dorian's gaze remained fixed on the screen long after the words had disappeared, his mind absorbing the reality of his situation with a slow, steady detachment. He had spent his life bending systems to his will, turning policies, markets, and entire industries into tools of his own making. Now, he was the tool. The system had adapted without him, and he was no longer the architect, he was the raw material.

The walls of the chamber were smooth, seamless, giving no indication of time or location. He had lost all external reference points. This was by design. Control required disorientation, the gradual erosion of self, until obedience became second nature, a conditioned response rather than a forced compliance. He knew this technique well. He had used similar methods in his own empire, manipulating consumer behaviors, crafting illusions of choice while ensuring that all paths led to the same predetermined outcome. They were not reinventing control. They were perfecting it.

The door to the chamber slid open without sound, and a woman entered, her expression neutral but assessing. She carried no visible weapon, no immediate threat, but the absolute confidence in her posture told him everything he needed to know. Power did not require brute force when it was absolute.

"Stand," she ordered.

He complied, rising with a measured precision that mirrored her own. He would not cower, but neither would he resist openly. Not yet.

She gestured for him to follow. He was led through a series of corridors, each identical to the last, the monotony itself a form of suppression. Every turn blurred into the next, ensuring that he could not map his surroundings, could not anchor himself in the physical world. Another layer of control.

Eventually, they arrived at a large, open chamber. The lighting was softer here, less sterile, but the intent remained the same. Several other men stood in formation, their postures rigid, their expressions blank. Some had already broken.

A central figure stood before them, a woman draped in tailored black, her presence more striking than any uniform. She studied them with an unwavering intensity before speaking.

"You misunderstand the nature of what has happened to you," she said, her voice steady but unyielding. "You believe you have been captured, that you have been reduced. But you have been liberated."

Silence. No one dared respond.

She continued. "You spent your lives in cages of your own making, believing power was something to be hoarded, that dominion over others was the truest expression of strength. That era has ended. You are no longer burdened by ambition, by status, by the need to compete. You exist now in perfect purpose. You will serve."

A man a few spaces down from Dorian flinched at the word, his breath catching in his throat. The woman turned her attention to him.

"You resist?" she asked, not with anger, but with mild curiosity.

The man clenched his jaw. "I was a senator. I shaped policy. I—"

She held up a hand, silencing him effortlessly. "You were nothing. A title does not make a man. A legacy does not excuse failure. The system you built was flawed, and now it is gone. You can either adapt to this world or be erased with the last remnants of the old one."

The senator hesitated. Then, slowly, he lowered his gaze.

Dorian did not move. This was the test. Compliance was not simply expected, it had to be internalized. The conditioning had begun, but the true breaking had yet to occur.

The woman stepped forward, glancing over the assembled men, her presence both commanding and patient. "You will be reclassified according to your abilities. Some of you will serve in labor, maintaining the structures of this new world. Some of you will be integrated into pleasure assignments, repurposed for the needs of those who now control your fate. And some of you..." She let the words hang, a deliberate pause meant to instill uncertainty. "Some of you will not be needed at all."

The air grew heavier, the unspoken threat saturating every breath. The knowledge that disposal was not a dramatic event, but a quiet, administrative decision, made it all the more potent. There would be no rebellions here. Only disappearances.

Dorian remained still, allowing the moment to pass over him without reaction. He had already seen the design of this system, divide, isolate, repurpose. There was no need for torture when the weight of survival itself was the most effective tool. They were not fighting them. They were dissolving them.

The session ended, and they were led away, separated into different sectors of the estate. Dorian was placed in an isolated chamber, the next stage of his integration waiting for him. He did not resist. He observed.

The game was not over. The rules had changed. But he was still playing.

Dorian sat in the cold silence of his chamber, his mind running over the words he had just heard. Some of you will not be needed at all. The phrase lingered, settling like an unspoken judgment. He had seen what happened to the men deemed unnecessary, the quiet efficiency with which they were removed, their very presence erased as though they had never existed.

No struggle. No ceremony. Just…gone.

A quiet chime rang from above, breaking the silence. A new message appeared on the wall screen, its meaning clear. Final assessments begin at dawn.

He exhaled slowly. The night would be long. Not because he feared what was coming, but because he knew this was his last chance to prepare.

He pushed his hands against the cool surface of the chamber wall, the tactile sensation grounding him for a moment. He had no way of knowing what the assessment entailed, but he understood its purpose. It was not a test he could pass; it was a decision already made, a predetermined outcome that had nothing to do with merit or worth. It was a reclassification. A reassignment of existence itself.

Some men would wake up tomorrow with a function. Others would never wake up at all.

Dorian sat back down, letting his mind work through possibilities. His former self, the man who dictated markets, controlled narratives, was gone. But the instincts, the ability to read between the lines, to analyze the power structure at play, those had not yet been stripped from him. Not entirely.

If there was a way to survive this, to move within it rather than be crushed by it, he would find it.

Dawn was coming. And with it, the moment of reckoning.

He stood again, pacing the small chamber, forcing his body into motion. He could feel his muscles tightening from inactivity, the stress accumulating in his limbs like unspent energy. This was how they broke men, not with brute force, but with containment, with silence, with the slow and steady erosion of will. He clenched his fists, then released them, reminding himself that submission was not survival. Adapting was.

He let his eyes scan the chamber, searching for anything, a weakness, an advantage, an opening in the system's flawless design. There was nothing. But that did not mean there wouldn't be.

The minutes stretched, uncounted, as he replayed every interaction, every word spoken. He needed to understand their methods, their rhythms, their expectations. There was always a pattern, and if he could find it, he could use it.

The walls were smooth, seamless, meant to make escape impossible. But Dorian was not thinking of escape. Not yet. First, he needed to become something they did not see coming.

Time had not yet run out.

Somewhere beyond this cell, someone had already decided what he would become. He had only until dawn to decide if they were right.

7
The List is Read

The chamber was silent except for the low hum of the overhead lights, a dull mechanical buzz that pulsed like a quiet, relentless heartbeat. The men stood in rigid lines, their postures stiff with uncertainty, exhaustion, and the weight of inevitability. No one spoke. No one dared to. The air was thick with something unnameable, a fear beyond panic, beyond rage. It was the fear of absolute nothingness, of becoming something less than a shadow.

Dorian's breath was slow, controlled, though he felt the tension in his body coil tighter with every passing second. His name had not been called yet, but it would be. They had stripped him of his clothes, of his possessions, of his dignity in ways both obvious and insidious. The weight of waiting was the final cruelty. Whatever came next would be the severing of the last thread tying him to his former self.

A row of women stood on a raised platform at the front of the chamber, their expressions unreadable, their presence exuding a quiet authority that needed no announcement. One of them stepped forward, a tablet in her hand, her voice smooth, unwavering.

"The designations are final. There are no appeals. The list is as follows."

The first name was called, followed by a short string of numbers. A man near the front flinched but remained still. A pause, and then: "Traitor."

Two figures stepped forward, their movements precise, mechanical. The man barely had time to react before they seized his arms, pulling him forward. He let out a strangled sound, not quite a protest, not quite a scream. He had been waiting for this, but the moment was still too fast, too final. He was dragged through the doors at the far end of the chamber, and the sound of his departure was swallowed by the oppressive silence that followed.

The next name was read, the next designation assigned. Labor Stock. The man assigned the role exhaled shakily but did not resist. He had been spared, in a sense. Hard labor meant existence, even if it was one defined by exhaustion and servitude.

The designations continued, each one a hammer strike. Useless Stock. Disposal. Entertainment. Entertainment. The word carried a different weight, one that hung in the air long after it was spoken, unspoken implications twisting in the silence.

Dorian's name was not called. Not yet. He listened as men were sorted, as their identities were ground down into classifications. The ones labeled Traitors were taken swiftly, with no chance to process the judgment. The Useless were led away with an efficiency that implied a destination no one wanted to think about. The Labor-bound remained, their fates clear, their exhaustion visible.

Then there were the ones marked for Entertainment.

Dorian knew what that meant. He had seen the carefully curated performances of the world's elite, the after-hours amusements that thrived behind closed doors. He had helped craft illusions of power, of control, of invulnerability. But this, this was not a curated spectacle. This was the turning of the tide, the inverse of every moment men like him had once dictated. They would not be killed outright. That would be too easy. They would be used.

His hands curled at his sides, a flicker of resistance rising and then vanishing beneath the weight of inevitability. They would call his name. Soon. The final severance was coming.

A pause, and then a name rang out, one that had once carried weight, prestige. Now, it was nothing more than another entry in a list.

"Dorian Thorne St. Claire."

His body did not betray him. He remained still, expression impassive, though every fiber of his being screamed against the moment. The pause stretched, and then the designation was spoken.

"Entertainment Stock."

There was no reaction in the room, no shift, no acknowledgment beyond the click of the tablet as the entry was confirmed. It was nothing. He was nothing. The name they had called was already fading, already being replaced by something else.

A second voice spoke, formal, detached. "Designation confirmed. John-1688A7-ICK2F."

Dorian did not flinch, though the words rang in his ears, final and absolute. He was no longer a name. He was a classification, an entry in a system that no longer acknowledged his past. The weight of it settled over him, pressing against his ribs like a cold, unseen hand.

He was turned away from the assembly, led toward a different door. Not the one that swallowed the Useless. Not the one that led to endless labor. This door led somewhere else, somewhere built for a different kind of submission. He stepped through without hesitation, because hesitation no longer mattered.

Behind him, the list continued to be read. The world moved forward, and he was already gone.

The hallway beyond the chamber was dimly lit, the walls sleek and seamless, betraying nothing of what lay ahead. His escort did not speak, did not so much as glance at him as they walked. Their silence was heavier than words, a calculated absence meant to strip him further of agency. He was not a man being led to a new life. He was a piece of inventory being transported.

Dorian's mind turned over the implications of his designation. Entertainment. It could mean many things, but he knew better than to expect comfort. The word itself was a branding, a final classification that ensured he would not disappear quickly or cleanly. He would be used, reshaped, molded into something else entirely. He had spent his life in rooms like this, rooms where decisions were made about people who never had a say. Now, he was the subject of that decision-making process.

They reached a door at the end of the hall, and it slid open without a sound. The room beyond was stark, functional. A single chair, a screen embedded in the wall, a sterile countertop lined with neatly arranged instruments. A woman stood waiting, dressed in the same severe uniform as the others, but there was something different about her. She looked at him directly, assessing him in a way that was not cruel but clinical, as if determining how best to proceed.

"Sit," she said.

He obeyed. There was no reason not to. The chair was solid, its material cool against his skin. The woman tapped something on the screen, and the room's lighting shifted slightly, the glow softening just enough to cast subtle shadows along the walls.

"Your identity has been processed," she said. "You are no longer Dorian Thorne St. Claire. You are John-1688A7-ICK2F. Your previous records, assets, and affiliations have been deleted."

He had expected as much. It did not make hearing it any less disorienting.

She turned the screen toward him, displaying a new profile, his face, stripped of all previous identifiers. Just the number. The designation. Nothing else.

"You will be trained for your role," she continued. "You will be conditioned to perform as required. Resistance will serve no purpose. Compliance ensures longevity."

Her tone was matter-of-fact, devoid of malice. This was not cruelty for cruelty's sake. This was simply how things were now.

Dorian met her gaze, held it. "And if I refuse?"

She did not blink. "You won't."

She tapped the screen again, and a new set of instructions appeared.

"The process begins now."

Dorian sat motionless in the chair, the cool material pressing against his skin as the woman across from him continued to study him. Her expression was unreadable, neither kind nor cruel, a neutrality that unnerved him more than open hostility would have. He had encountered many people in his life who had wielded power, who had dictated fates, but they had always exuded a personal interest, whether it was greed, ambition, or a perverse sense of righteousness. This woman had none of that. She was merely enacting a process, as detached from it as a machine executing its function.

She tapped the screen again, and a quiet chime sounded through the room. A second door to the side of the chamber slid open, revealing another figure. This one was a man, though he did not carry himself as the other men Dorian had seen here. He was taller, lean, with sharp features and an economy of movement that suggested training. His gaze flicked to Dorian for a brief second before he turned to the woman.

"Processing has begun?" the man asked, his voice smooth, efficient.

The woman nodded. "Final phase. You may proceed."

The man stepped forward, stopping just in front of Dorian, close enough that Dorian could see the faint lines of old scars running along the backs of his hands. "Stand."

Dorian obeyed, suppressing the instinct to hesitate. He was aware that every action now was a test, every movement observed and analyzed. The man gestured toward the newly opened doorway, and Dorian stepped through without protest. The hallway beyond was dimly lit, narrow, leading toward another chamber. He did not look back.

The new room was larger than the last, though just as sterile. A mirrored wall stretched along one side, the kind that only reflected on one end. He could feel unseen eyes on him. At the center of the room was a circular platform, slightly raised, with what looked like embedded sensors in its surface.

"Stand in the center," the man instructed.

Dorian did as he was told. The moment his feet touched the platform, a low hum filled the air, and faint lines of light traced the edges of the structure. He felt something shift beneath him, a barely perceptible adjustment in weight. The man stepped away, moving toward a panel on the wall. The woman, who had followed them in, stood just beyond the threshold, watching.

"Identity confirmation complete," the man announced. "Subject is stable. Ready for conditioning protocols."

A sharp click echoed in the room, and the lights changed, darkening the walls while casting an eerie, bluish glow over the platform. Dorian tensed but did not move. He understood the purpose of this moment. It was not about compliance alone. It was about control, how quickly they could dismantle whatever resistance remained inside him. How easily they could shape him into what they required.

"Stage one: Sensory recalibration," the man said.

The platform pulsed, a wave of energy flowing through his body, not painful but invasive. It was a subtle shift, one that made his skin prickle, his equilibrium tilt slightly. He clenched his jaw, forcing himself to remain still.

"Subject response: Minimal," the man noted, making an entry on his device. "Increasing frequency."

The sensation intensified, and Dorian felt his perception alter slightly, as if the boundaries of the room had subtly warped. A test. They were probing, searching for thresholds. He focused on his breathing, steadying himself.

The process continued, each adjustment bringing a new layer of disorientation. His sense of time fragmented, stretched, compressed. At some point, they introduced auditory distortions, whispers that seemed to come from nowhere, familiar voices spliced with alien tones. Then came the flashes of images across the mirrored wall, too brief to fully process but carrying an undeniable weight. His own face, altered. His own voice, saying things he had never spoken.

"Subject maintains stability," the man observed. "Notable resistance to initial phases. Proceeding to cognitive reframe."

A new sequence began, and this time, Dorian felt the shift internally rather than externally. The whispers became clearer, forming sentences. Some of them were his own thoughts, ones he had never voiced aloud. Others were foreign, unfamiliar beliefs woven in among them. He recognized the technique. It was the kind of psychological engineering he had seen used in interrogation chambers, in corporate training programs designed to rewire an employee's loyalty.

They were rewriting him.

It was slow, insidious. There was no single point where the shift happened, no line he could draw to say, *this is where I lost myself.* It was in the layering, the careful weaving of memory and suggestion, until his own recollections no longer felt entirely his.

"Subject is adapting," the man noted. "Phase one complete. Transitioning to behavioral imprinting."

Dorian exhaled, steadying himself. He had expected something brutal, something forceful. Instead, this was patient, meticulous. They were not trying to break him. They were erasing him piece by piece, until the only thing left was what they had shaped him into.

The lights shifted again, and the platform powered down. The man stepped forward, studying him with a clinical detachment. "You are adjusting well. The next stages will be easier."

Dorian did not respond. He knew the game. Knew that if he spoke, it would be another metric to be recorded, another piece of him surrendered. He had spent his life controlling the narrative. Now, he was the subject of it, and the only power he had left was in how much of himself he allowed them to see.

"Escort him to holding," the man instructed. "Session resumes at first cycle."

The woman nodded, stepping forward to lead him away. He followed without hesitation. The walls of the corridor blurred slightly as they walked, whether from exhaustion or the lingering effects of the session, he could not tell. But as he moved, one thought settled in his mind, steady and undeniable.

He was not broken. Not yet.

Dorian was led down another corridor, his steps steady but measured, his mind working through the fractures of what had just been done to him. The process had begun, but it had not finished. He could still feel himself there, still present, still aware, though he knew that was the point of the initial phases. They did not expect to break him in a day. They wanted to rewrite him, slow enough that he wouldn't notice the moment he ceased to be who he had been. That was the real weapon, not pain, not violence, but time, the slow dissolution of self.

He was placed in a new room, larger than the first, but still absent of anything unnecessary. A simple cot, a mirror that was certainly two-way, and a wall screen that was blank for now but would no doubt come to life when they were ready. The woman who had escorted him inside said nothing. She pressed something on her tablet, scanning him one last time before turning and walking out, the door sealing behind her. No locks, no visible bolts. The kind of door designed to remind you that you had no need to escape because there was nowhere to go.

Dorian sat down on the cot, exhaling slowly, his hands pressed against his thighs. He did not pace, did not show outward agitation. That would be expected, noted, categorized. Instead, he remained still, listening. The quiet was purposeful, designed to make him feel alone, but he knew he wasn't. They were watching. Observing. Waiting to see how he settled into this new existence. He leaned back against the wall, eyes fixed on the blank screen. It would begin again soon.

The screen flickered to life. At first, there was nothing but static, a subtle hum that vibrated through the room. Then, an image formed, his own face, but altered. Softer in some ways, unfamiliar in others. A version of himself that did not quite belong to him. His own voice followed, though the words were not his own. They were pieces of old interviews, recordings he had given in the past, but stitched together into a different narrative. One where he spoke of service, of duty, of understanding his place in the world. It was eerie, how seamlessly it had been done, how convincingly his own voice betrayed him.

The sequence repeated, shifting slightly each time. The words became less foreign, the cadence more familiar, the intent settling into the spaces between his thoughts. He knew the method. Repetition was the foundation of all belief. It was not about immediate acceptance. It was about exposure, about normalizing the idea until resistance faded, until the mind adjusted. And yet, knowing the method did not make him immune to it. He could feel the pressure of it against his consciousness, the way it nudged at the corners of his certainty. He forced himself to hold on to the facts, this was a construct, a carefully designed manipulation. But even facts could be worn down given enough time.

The screen went dark again, the room falling back into silence. But the echo of his own words, twisted into something new, remained in the air. A test, but also a foundation. This was not about obedience. This was about reshaping his very sense of self.

He inhaled deeply, counting his breaths. They would return soon. The next stage would begin. And when it did, he needed to be ready.

The door opened without warning, and two figures stepped inside. The man from before, the one who had overseen the first phase, and a new woman, taller, her presence more pronounced. She carried herself with an ease that spoke of control, of a certainty that had been tested and proven unshakable. She regarded him with interest, though not the kind that suggested curiosity. It was the kind of interest one had when evaluating the reliability of a machine.

"You're adapting well," she said, stepping closer. "Better than expected. But you already know that, don't you?"

Dorian met her gaze, saying nothing.

"You understand the process," she continued. "You've studied it before, in a different context. You know what's happening. That's why you're resisting, not in the way we normally see, but in the way that matters. It's impressive. But ultimately, irrelevant."

She moved past him, tapping something on the wall screen. It flickered back to life, showing not his face this time, but the faces of others, men who had already been processed, their expressions vacant but serene. They were not broken, not in the way most would expect. They had been restructured, molded into something that no longer struggled. No longer needed to.

"You see, the difference between resistance and acceptance is time," she said. "The mind is not built to fight forever. It needs stability, predictability. Eventually, even the strongest minds settle into what is given to them."

The man beside her spoke for the first time. "And you will, too."

Dorian did not respond, but they did not expect him to. This was still part of the preparation, the groundwork being laid. They did not need an immediate response. They needed the awareness to take root, the inevitability of what was coming to settle in. They were not forcing compliance. They were allowing him to come to it himself. And that was far more dangerous than any act of violence.

The woman gestured toward the screen. "Watch," she instructed. And he did.

The images played, one after another. Men he had known, men who had been powerful, influential, reduced to something else entirely. They spoke in calm voices, their words measured, their tones devoid of anything but acceptance. They explained the system, their roles, their understanding of what had been done to them. And they did not resist. Not anymore.

One by one, they spoke, and Dorian felt the weight of it pressing against him, the slow, inexorable pull of normalization. It would not happen today, or tomorrow. But it would happen. That was the truth of it. That was the reality he was up against.

The screen faded to black once more, and the woman turned back to him. "We will speak again soon," she said, and then she and the man were gone, leaving Dorian alone in the silence once more.

He sat still, his hands resting on his thighs, his gaze locked on the now-empty screen. His mind turned over everything he had seen, everything he had heard. He was still himself. But for how much longer?

He had always believed that power was about control, about shaping narratives. But now, he understood something else. True power was not about dictating what people believed. It was about making them believe it themselves.

And that was what they were doing to him now.

Dorian sat unmoving in the silence that followed. The weight of what he had seen, of what had been presented to him, pressed heavily against his thoughts, an unseen force attempting to settle into the spaces of his mind. He was not broken. Not yet. But he had seen how easily it happened, how methodically they unraveled the men before him, how seamless the transformation became once the mind stopped resisting. The process was not about force, it was about inevitability. And inevitability was difficult to fight.

The screen remained dark, the room absent of anything that might provide a distraction. There was no clock, no window, nothing to gauge the passing of time except his own breathing. That was intentional. They wanted him to exist only in this moment, untethered from any sense of external reality. He did not know how long he had been here, only that the boundaries of before and after had begun to blur.

The door slid open again. The woman from before re-entered, her presence as composed and deliberate as ever. Behind her, a second figure entered, another man, though different from the first. He was younger, softer around the edges, but still carrying the same quiet authority. He looked at Dorian without expression, and Dorian knew instantly, this was another step in the process. Another layer of control being applied.

The woman gestured toward the chair across from him. "Sit."

Dorian remained where he was. He was not yet ready to surrender to reflex, to automatic obedience. He wanted them to know that he still had a choice, even if it was just the illusion of one.

She waited, unbothered, unmoved by his small act of defiance. Then, she tilted her head slightly. "You misunderstand," she said simply. "This is not about force. It never has been. You will sit because you want to."

Dorian held her gaze for a moment longer before shifting forward, lowering himself into the chair with slow deliberation. He would not let them frame this as victory. He was still here. He was still himself.

The younger man sat as well, studying him with a measured calm. "You're holding onto something," he said after a beat. "Something you think is still yours." Dorian said nothing.

The man continued, undeterred. "It's always the same. The belief that resistance means something. That you are an exception. That you, unlike the others, will endure."

Dorian met his gaze, silent.

The man sighed, leaning back. "You don't realize that resistance is built into the system. You are expected to fight, for a time. Expected to believe that you can hold onto yourself. It is part of the process. A necessary step in what comes next."

Dorian exhaled slowly, considering the words. They were meant to disarm him, to plant doubt in the foundation of his certainty. He could feel the weight of them pressing inward, subtle, patient, waiting to take root.

The woman watched the exchange without interruption, then reached for a small device on the table. She pressed something, and the screen lit up once more. This time, it was not unfamiliar faces. It was him.

Dorian stared at the image of himself, distorted slightly, just enough to be unsettling. He was speaking, but he had no memory of ever saying the words. They were his voice, his cadence, but not his thoughts. The screen flickered, shifting between different recordings, different moments, each one more convincing than the last. If he had not known better, if he had not been certain of his own mind, he might have believed them.

"You see?" the younger man said. "We are not here to make you something else. We are here to help you understand what you already are."

Dorian forced himself to hold steady, to ground himself in the knowledge that this was manipulation, a carefully crafted attempt to erode him. But even as he reminded himself of that truth, he felt the creeping awareness of how easily the mind could be led astray. The more something was repeated, the more it became familiar. And familiarity bred acceptance.

The woman set the device down. "We will continue," she said, standing. "You are adjusting well."

The door slid open once more, and she exited. The younger man remained seated for a moment longer, watching Dorian with an almost thoughtful expression.

"Do you know why this works?" he asked finally. "Not because we force compliance. Not because we instill fear. But because we provide certainty. You've spent your entire life chasing power, thinking that was control. But control is an illusion. True certainty is knowing your place in the world, and we are giving that to you."

Dorian's jaw tightened, but he said nothing. The man stood, moving toward the exit.

"We will continue," he repeated, echoing the woman's words. "Rest while you can." And then he was gone.

Dorian was alone again, but the silence no longer felt the same. It was heavier now, filled with the lingering echoes of everything that had been said, everything that had been shown to him. He leaned back against the wall, staring at the dark screen, his mind running over the conversations, the images, the carefully constructed unraveling of who he was.

They were right about one thing. Resistance alone was not enough. He could fight as long as he wanted, but they had time. They would wait. They would press forward, patient and unyielding, until the moment came when he no longer knew if he was resisting at all.

His breathing was steady, measured. His pulse even. But inside, he felt the edges of himself fraying, just slightly, just enough to know that if he did not find a way to counter this, to root himself in something stronger than defiance, he would eventually become exactly what they wanted him to be.

He would not break. But he would need more than willpower to remain whole.

The door remained shut, the screen dark. He closed his eyes, forcing himself to recall memories, moments that belonged only to him. He would hold onto them, for now. For as long as he could.

ACT II

THE BREAKING OF MEN (SUBMISSION OR DEATH)

8
The Auction House

Dorian stood in the holding chamber, the sterile glow of overhead lights flattening the depth of everything around him. The room was filled with other men, all of them stripped down to the same uniform neutrality, plain, featureless clothing that erased any remaining sense of identity. There were no names here, only numbers. He had been processed, cataloged, and designated. Now, he was simply an entry in a ledger, a commodity awaiting sale.

A heavy silence lingered over the group, thick with the weight of realization. The others avoided eye contact, some staring at the floor, others at the walls, anywhere but at each other. Dorian had once seen men in this same state of quiet panic in corporate boardrooms when their empires crumbled around them. Now, there were no more titles to shield them, no safety nets of wealth or influence. They were stripped of their illusions, and with it, their power.

A low chime rang through the room, signaling movement. One by one, they were led out into the hall beyond, their escorts impassive. Dorian felt the press of hands against his arm, firm but not aggressive. He followed without protest. He knew better than to resist now; there was no resistance. There was only what came next.

The hallway spilled into a larger chamber, one with a low, elevated platform at its center. A series of tiered seats encircled the stage, occupied entirely by women. They sat in relaxed poses, some leaning forward in interest, others making idle conversation. Their attention wasn't on the men being ushered in, not yet. This was routine for them, something they had seen before.

Dorian had attended auctions before, though never from this side of the transaction. He had been among the buyers, the powerful, the untouchable. He had seen the thrill in the faces of those who could afford to treat human lives as investments, as entertainment. Now, he was the object of that gaze. The reversal was deliberate. Calculated.

A woman at the front, dressed in deep red, rose to address the room. "The next lot is a collection of high-value assets," she announced, her voice carrying easily across the space. "Each has been evaluated and categorized for entertainment purposes. Their previous designations are irrelevant. What matters now is their function."

Dorian felt the shift in attention as the women in the audience turned their focus toward the men standing in a neat line. He kept his expression neutral, though he knew this was the moment they were expected to react, to shrink, to resist, to betray some flicker of desperation. He did none of those things. He knew how optics worked. He had crafted them his entire life. The only thing left to control was how they saw him.

One by one, the men were brought forward, their profiles read aloud, their new designations announced. Some were categorized as performers, others as companions, and some, those who failed to meet whatever unspoken criteria existed, were dismissed entirely. There was no indication of what happened to those who were not selected.

When Dorian's name was called, or rather, when his number was read, he stepped forward without hesitation. The woman in red glanced at the screen beside her, scanning his profile. "This one," she said, turning to the audience, "was once considered among the elite. A former media magnate, a power player in corporate influence. He has been reassigned to entertainment."

A ripple of interest moved through the crowd. A woman in the front row tilted her head. "He doesn't look broken yet," she observed.

The auctioneer smiled. "That is part of the appeal."

Dorian remained still as the bidding began. The numbers rose quickly, not because of necessity, but because of amusement. He was no longer a man; he was an object of spectacle. The final price was irrelevant, it was about the act of acquisition, about the performance of power.

The bidding war ended as suddenly as it began. A number was called, a final confirmation given. Dorian did not turn to see who had placed the winning bid. It did not matter. His fate had been decided in the space of minutes, his worth reduced to an exchange of figures. He had once built an empire on valuation, on market strategies and negotiation tactics. Now, he was the commodity being assessed.

A quiet chime signaled the end of the transaction, and he was led away. His buyer had not stepped forward, had not introduced herself. That, too, was intentional. He would learn his fate in time. Until then, he was simply property in transit.

The door sealed behind him, closing out the sound of laughter and casual conversation from the auction hall. He did not allow himself to react, not yet. There was no point in wasting energy on what could not be changed. Instead, he let his thoughts settle, his mind working through the next step.

Because there was always a next step. No matter how far he had fallen, no matter how much had been taken, the game was never over.

Not yet.

Dorian was led down a corridor that stretched longer than seemed possible, its muted lighting casting elongated shadows along the floor. The footsteps of his escort were measured, unhurried, a stark contrast to the rushed, clipped paces of the men he had once commanded in his former life. There was no urgency here. His fate had already been sealed, and he was no longer an individual requiring special treatment. He was cargo, an investment that had already been paid for. The transaction was complete, and now all that remained was the delivery.

The silence between him and his escort was absolute, but not empty. It carried with it an air of unspoken expectation, the weight of something inevitable pressing against the stillness. Dorian did not ask where he was being taken, nor did he attempt to engage in whatever strained, false civility might have existed between captor and captive. He had learned early that silence was the only currency left to him, and he spent it wisely.

The corridor eventually ended at a door, sleek and unmarked, indistinguishable from the many others they had passed. The escort did not hesitate before placing a hand against the panel beside it, triggering the mechanism that slid it open. The room beyond was not what Dorian had expected. He had assumed something clinical, a space designed for the systematic breaking of men like him, a sterile holding pen to strip away whatever dignity still clung to those who had not yet fully accepted their place. Instead, the room was opulent, disturbingly so. Soft lighting, a thickly woven rug beneath his feet, furnishings that were understated in their luxury. It was not meant to be welcoming, but it was meant to unsettle.

A woman sat at a low table near the center of the space, her posture relaxed but deliberate. She did not look up immediately, instead taking her time as she finished what she was reading on a thin, illuminated tablet. When she finally lifted her gaze to meet his, it was not with the clinical detachment of those who had processed him. There was something else there, an appraisal, yes, but layered beneath it, something more calculated.

"You may leave us," she said without looking at the escort. The guard obeyed without hesitation, exiting as soundlessly as he had arrived, the door sealing shut behind him. Dorian did not move, did not shift under her gaze, though he was keenly aware of how this moment had been designed. She had waited. Had let him stand there just long enough to make him aware that she controlled every aspect of the interaction, from the timing to the silence that stretched between them.

She set the tablet down, leaning back slightly. "You expected something different," she observed, her voice smooth but with the faintest edge of amusement.

Dorian's expression did not shift. "Should I?"

She tilted her head slightly, considering him. "That depends. What did you think would happen once the auction was over?"

There was no point in lying. She already knew the answer. "I thought I'd be thrown into some training program, conditioned further until I was whatever you needed me to be."

The amusement in her expression deepened, but it did not reach her eyes. "And you assume that isn't happening now?"

Dorian did not respond immediately. Instead, he let the silence stretch just long enough to see if she would fill it. She did not.

"What do you want from me?" he asked finally.

She smiled then, not a warm smile, not meant to reassure, but a measured expression designed to remind him of his position. "That remains to be seen."

She stood, moving toward a side table where a decanter and two glasses sat, untouched. She poured a drink, her movements slow and deliberate, then held up the glass in offering. "Would you like one?"

Dorian did not move. He understood the test in the question. He had spent his life studying these moments, had used them himself against those he needed to control. The drink was not a kindness; it was a measure. To accept would be to acknowledge civility, to engage in the illusion that there was a choice to be made. To refuse would be to defy the premise of this interaction entirely.

After a long moment, he stepped forward and took the glass.

The woman watched him, nodding slightly as if his choice had told her something she had been waiting to confirm. She took a sip of her own drink, then gestured to a chair opposite the one she had occupied before. "Sit."

Dorian did not hesitate this time. The chair was comfortable, but he did not allow himself to relax. She studied him as she took another measured sip, then set the glass down. "You intrigue me," she said simply.

Dorian did not react. He knew better than to ask why.

She continued without prompting. "Most men who come through the auction still cling to something, whether it's delusion, arrogance, or fear, they all have something left to lose." She leaned forward slightly. "You don't seem to."

Dorian met her gaze evenly. "Because I understand what's happening to me?"

Her smile was faint. "Because you haven't broken the way they expected you to."

Dorian allowed himself a slow breath, careful not to betray anything beyond what was necessary. "And what is it that you expect?"

She studied him for a moment longer, then leaned back. "I suppose we'll find out."

Another pause, then she gestured toward the door. "You will stay here. Your movements will be restricted for now, but within reason. You will be observed, but I don't think I need to remind you that attempting anything foolish would not serve you well."

Dorian inclined his head slightly. "Of course."

She watched him for another beat before standing. "Get some rest," she said, then moved toward the door, pausing just before she stepped through it. "Tomorrow, we begin."

Then she was gone, leaving Dorian alone in the opulence of his cage, the weight of her final words settling over him like a warning he had yet to understand.

Dorian woke to the soft hum of the ventilation system and the filtered light seeping in through the edges of the window covering. The air smelled different, tinged with something faintly floral, unfamiliar yet calculated. Every element of the space was designed with precision, from the texture of the sheets to the subtle temperature regulation, comfort without warmth, a luxury that was meant to disarm rather than soothe.

He sat up slowly, his body instinctively taking stock of itself. No visible restraints. No obvious monitoring devices, though he knew better than to assume he was unwatched. His muscles ached, though not from exertion. It was the weight of stillness, of being forced into a condition of waiting, the slow erosion of agency through controlled inaction. He had spent his life in motion, making decisions, dictating outcomes. Now, he was adrift in someone else's current.

The door opened without preamble, and she entered, the same woman from the night before. She moved with an economy of motion that spoke of deliberate intent. No unnecessary gestures, no wasted energy. She carried herself like someone who had never had to demand authority, it had been granted to her the moment she stepped into a room.

"You slept," she observed, more statement than question.

Dorian didn't bother responding. She already knew the answer, just as she knew that his waking had been monitored, his behavior studied even in unconsciousness.

She sat across from him, adjusting the cuff of her sleeve as though the meeting itself was incidental. "You've been assigned to me. That much you know. What you don't know is what that means." She paused, letting the silence stretch just long enough to underline the weight of her words. "So let's clarify it now."

Dorian remained still, waiting. He had spent years negotiating with people who prided themselves on controlling the flow of conversation. He understood the game. The first mistake was to engage too early, to give too much before you understood the full scope of the rules.

She continued, unbothered by his silence. "You are not here to be broken. If that were the goal, you would already have been processed differently. You are not here to be discarded. You are here because you are useful. The only question is whether or not you will recognize that soon enough to take advantage of it."

A subtle shift in her tone, the faintest suggestion of invitation. Not an offer, not yet, but a thread left untied, waiting to be pulled.

Dorian met her gaze. "And how exactly am I useful?"

Her lips curved slightly, though it was not quite a smile. "You built influence on perception. You understood how to manufacture narratives, how to turn public sentiment like an algorithm. You shaped entire industries around belief. That is not a skill that vanishes simply because your position has changed."

A beat of silence stretched between them. The room felt smaller, though neither of them had moved.

"You want me to do the same for you," he said finally.

"I want you to recognize that you are still in play," she corrected. "The only thing that has changed is your vantage point."

Dorian leaned back slightly, considering. She was offering something, though veiled. Not a restoration of his past, but a position within something new. And yet, there was no illusion that he was anything but property. That was the crux of the dynamic being established, he could be useful, but never equal. He could shape narratives, but not his own.

She studied him, her expression unreadable. "I don't expect an answer now. You'll come to it on your own."

She rose, adjusting the cuff of her sleeve once more. "You will be given more freedom than most. Within limits. Explore, familiarize yourself. But do not mistake proximity to power for ownership of it."

With that, she left, the door sealing shut behind her with the soft finality of a cell door, no matter how opulent the surroundings might be.

Dorian remained seated, staring at the space where she had been. He exhaled slowly, his mind working through the implications of what had just transpired. This was not about immediate compliance. It was about erosion, about planting the suggestion of collaboration and letting it grow until it seemed like choice.

He pushed himself to his feet, stretching out the stiffness in his shoulders before moving toward the only other door in the room. It opened at his approach, revealing a hallway that was both unfamiliar and unsettlingly designed. No clear exits, no obvious pathways to anything beyond the controlled environment they had constructed for him.

As he stepped forward, he realized the truth of what she had said, he was not broken, not yet. But the question was no longer about whether he would resist. It was about how long he could endure before resistance became indistinguishable from adaptation.

And whether, in the end, that distinction would matter at all.

Dorian moved through the corridors with a calculated calm, his eyes taking in every detail, subtle security measures, the quiet hum of surveillance, the lack of windows offering any real view beyond this curated reality. He understood the purpose behind this, control was not exerted through brute force but through precision, through a careful balance of perceived autonomy and unavoidable restriction.

The hallways branched out in patterns that felt intentional, leading him past rooms that hinted at function without fully revealing their purpose. He caught glimpses of others, men like him, dressed identically, their expressions vacant or wary, depending on how far along they were in their own respective processes. He did not stop, did not engage. It was clear this was not a space designed for unstructured interaction.

A quiet chime echoed through the corridor, and a door ahead of him slid open. It led to a larger room, its design more open than the chamber he had been assigned to. The walls were lined with shelves, filled with books, data tablets, and artifacts that spoke of curated history. At the center of the room stood a seating area arranged around a glass table. A woman was already seated there, waiting for him.

She was different from the one who had purchased him. There was no subtlety to her presence, no layers of carefully veiled control. She was direct, her gaze sharp as she gestured for him to sit across from her. He recognized her type immediately, an evaluator, someone who functioned not on power alone but on the ability to measure, to dismantle and restructure.

"You are here because we need to determine how useful you truly are," she stated, foregoing any pretense of small talk. "Not all who are chosen remain chosen. Some become assets. Some become obsolete."

Dorian did not react, did not give her anything beyond his controlled expression. "And how do you decide?"

"Through demonstration," she replied. "You built influence on perception, controlled the flow of information. We require that skill, but stripped of your own agenda. We will see if that is possible."

The screen embedded in the table flickered to life, showing a live feed of a panel of individuals discussing policy, their voices muted but their gestures sharp, practiced. It was a performance, one he had seen replicated in various forms across industries, across governments. The information being shaped rather than presented, the conversation maneuvered rather than explored.

"Rewrite the narrative," she instructed. "Take what is being said and make it into what should be heard. You have five minutes."

Dorian exhaled slowly, fingers tapping against the surface of the table as he analyzed the discussion. The key was not to fabricate but to redirect, to alter without allowing the shift to be seen as artificial. He had done this a thousand times before, turning crises into triumphs, shaping public perception with a precision that made truth irrelevant. And yet, this was different. This was not for his gain, not for his empire, but for them.

Still, the skill remained. He adjusted the framing of the discussion, his words precise, his changes seamless. The panel's dialogue was rewritten in real-time, altered to push forward an angle that maintained the illusion of free discourse while ensuring the outcome had already been decided. He finished just as the five-minute mark was reached, his revised version now displaying on the screen.

The woman watched, studying both the content and the method. She gave nothing away, no immediate approval or disapproval. Then, after a long silence, she nodded. "Acceptable. We will continue."

Dorian did not react outwardly, but he understood the implication. He had passed this round, but the evaluation was far from over. He was still a test subject, his value conditional, his existence within this framework a fragile construct that could be shattered at any time.

The woman stood, gesturing toward the door. "Return to your quarters. You will be given further instruction when necessary."

He rose, moving toward the exit without hesitation. As the door sealed behind him, he let out a slow breath, his mind processing everything that had just transpired.

They wanted him functional, but on their terms. The question now was not whether he could perform, it was whether he could navigate this system without losing what remained of himself in the process.

And whether, in the end, that choice would even matter.

Dorian walked the same corridors back, but this time, they felt smaller. The world around him had not physically changed, yet the space between his options seemed to shrink. There was no escape here, only movement within parameters. That was the game they were playing, and he had spent his entire life mastering systems exactly like this one. Only now, he was on the wrong side of it.

His quarters were as he left them, untouched, the illusion of privacy maintained. He sat at the edge of the cot, rolling his shoulders, forcing the tension from his muscles. This, too, was part of their method, give him just enough comfort to keep him from breaking too soon, but never enough to let him believe he had control.

His gaze drifted to the door. Would it open if he tried? Probably. That was the trick of it. They would let him walk, let him see, let him believe he had choices, but none of those choices would ever lead to freedom. They were not keeping him locked in. They were keeping him occupied.

His fingers tapped against his thigh, the movement rhythmic, grounding. He needed to think, to strategize. This was not about brute force; that would be the first mistake. He was not a prisoner in the traditional sense. He was an asset, at least for now, and that gave him a narrow sliver of leverage. They wanted him to adapt, to integrate. That meant there was room to maneuver.

But he had to be careful. Too much resistance, and he would be discarded. Too much cooperation, and he would become exactly what they wanted him to be. The balance was razor-thin, and he had no margin for error.

He exhaled slowly, closing his eyes. This was the long game now. He had played it before, only now, the stakes were himself.

He would not be erased. Not yet.

9
The Reeducation Centers Open

Dorian was moved in silence, his escort leading him through yet another set of sterile corridors. The walls were identical to those he had seen before, smooth, seamless, devoid of any distinct markings or indications of place. The lack of distinction was part of the strategy. Without a sense of location, there could be no orientation, no direction except forward, toward whatever they had planned for him next.

He did not ask where they were going. He knew by now that questions would receive no answers. He had tested those limits early on, and in return, he had been met only with the quiet, unshaken discipline of his handlers. They were not there to inform. They were there to deliver. And so he walked, the tension settling into his muscles as they approached a door wider than the others, reinforced, its edges glowing faintly with embedded sensors.

It slid open without a sound.

The room beyond was vast, more industrial than any space he had been placed in before. The lighting was dimmer here, casting elongated shadows over the polished floor. Men were already inside, some seated at long tables arranged in perfect symmetry, others standing in separate formations, their postures varying between forced compliance and simmering defiance. Dorian recognized some of them, former executives, politicians, men who had once been untouchable. Now, they were indistinguishable from one another, clad in the same muted uniforms, their pasts reduced to nothing more than whispered memories.

A voice rang out, sharp and impassive. "Take your place."

Dorian did not immediately move, his eyes sweeping across the space. It was designed to resemble a training facility, but not the kind that shaped leaders. This was not an arena for growth, it was a chamber for submission. Everything, from the positioning of the tables to the calculated spacing of the guards along the walls, reinforced the unspoken command: Obey, or be removed.

He stepped forward, joining a row of men who stood with their hands at their sides. Some of them glanced at him, measuring, assessing. He did not acknowledge them. His focus remained on the woman at the front of the room, the one who had given the order. She was different from the others he had encountered, her stance less clinical, her demeanor marked with a certain detached amusement. She had seen men like him before, and she had no illusions about what was coming next.

"You have all been brought here for one reason," she said. "Correction."

The word hung in the air, as heavy as the silence that followed. No one responded. Some of the men had already learned not to speak unless prompted. Others were simply waiting, unwilling to be the first to break the silence.

She took a slow step forward, her gaze sweeping across them. "Your past lives no longer exist. Your titles, your wealth, your influence, none of it holds meaning anymore. What matters now is your willingness to understand that."

Dorian did not look away. He recognized this speech for what it was: the prelude to conditioning. It was meant to instill the idea that the past was irrelevant, that the only reality that mattered was the one being imposed upon them now. The technique was old, but effective. Break the mind, and the body would follow.

"Some of you will adapt quickly," she continued, her voice even. "Others will resist. And those who resist will learn that resistance has consequences."

The room remained still, but the tension had thickened, the unspoken weight of her words settling over them.

She gestured, and a group of guards moved forward. They stopped in front of the first row of men, their expressions devoid of emotion. Then, without warning, they struck.

Dorian heard the sharp sound of flesh meeting flesh, the short, muffled gasps of impact. He did not turn to look. He had expected this. Compliance was never voluntary, it was beaten into place, submission carved out of flesh and bone until obedience was the only path left. He stood still as the blows continued, listening to the stifled cries, the sound of bodies crumpling to the floor. He did not flinch, did not react.

And then it was his turn.

The guard in front of him did not hesitate. The first blow landed against his ribs, hard enough to send a sharp pulse of pain radiating through his torso. He remained upright, his breath escaping between clenched teeth, but he did not fall. The second strike came faster, aimed lower, forcing him to brace against the impact. He felt the familiar sting of bruising beneath his skin, but he did not bend. Not yet.

The woman watched, expression unchanged. "You believe pain makes you stronger," she said, almost conversationally. That is what you told yourself, isn't it? That suffering builds resilience."

Dorian swallowed the taste of copper in his mouth, breathing through his nose. He did not answer.

"Pain does not make you stronger," she continued. "It simply reveals what you truly are."

The next strike landed against his jaw, sharp and clean. His head snapped to the side, but he caught himself before he staggered. He straightened slowly, his breath steady. He would not give them what they wanted. He had survived worse than this.

She stepped closer, tilting her head slightly as she examined him. "You think this is about endurance. That if you hold out long enough, you win. But this is not a battle. This is recalibration. And whether you realize it or not, the process has already begun."

He met her gaze, his body aching with the effort of remaining upright. He did not reply.

"Take him back," she ordered, turning away. "He will learn soon enough."

The guards seized his arms, leading him back toward the corridor from which he had come. Dorian did not resist. His steps were steady, his breath controlled. He knew this was only the beginning.

And he knew they were waiting for him to break.

But they would have to wait longer.

Dorian was deposited into a holding cell, the door sliding shut behind him with a quiet finality. The space was small, sparsely furnished, a cot bolted to the wall, a steel basin, a single overhead light that cast a dim glow against the sterile white walls. The scent of antiseptic clung to the air, a subtle reminder that pain here was routine, expected, and cleansed away without sentiment.

He remained standing, his ribs aching with each breath, his jaw stiff where the last blow had landed. He had learned long ago how to pace his breathing, how to distribute pain so it did not consume him entirely. This was not the first time he had been reduced to something less than human in the eyes of those who thought they could wield power without consequence. But this time was different. This time, he had no empire to return to, no contingency plan waiting in the shadows. The only thing left was himself.

A panel on the opposite wall flickered to life, the screen embedded within it blinking as if rousing from a dormant state. Dorian watched without moving as a familiar face appeared, her, the one who had spoken to him in the training hall, the one who had called this process 'recalibration.' She studied him for a moment, her expression neutral.

"You are processing slower than expected," she remarked, her voice even, detached. "That is not unusual, but it is inefficient."

Dorian did not respond. Silence, he had learned, was the only real currency he had left.

She did not seem bothered by his lack of reaction. "You believe that endurance is resistance," she continued. "That if you withstand the conditions placed upon you, you are somehow unchanged. That is a misconception we encounter often."

Still, he did not speak.

She sighed, as if disappointed, though he suspected it was for effect rather than genuine feeling. "Your designation requires mental reconditioning in addition to physical recalibration. We will begin today."

The screen flickered off before he could gauge what that meant. A moment later, the door slid open once more, and two figures entered, guards, impassive and efficient. They did not speak as they gestured for him to follow.

Dorian moved without resistance. He had no reason to fight them now. Not yet.

He was led down a different corridor this time, one that was noticeably quieter. The walls were unadorned, the silence oppressive. It reminded him of the executive offices he once controlled, places where decisions were made behind soundproofed walls, where the most significant actions left no echo.

They entered a chamber larger than his cell but just as bare. A single chair sat in the center of the room, positioned beneath an array of monitors suspended from the ceiling. The screens displayed nothing yet, their black surfaces smooth and waiting.

The guards left without instruction, the door sealing behind them with an air of finality. Then, the screens came to life.

Dorian saw himself.

Not as he was now, bruised and stripped down to an anonymous shell, but as he had been, the media mogul, the man who shaped elections, who dictated narratives, who could, with a single broadcast, shift public opinion like a tide. The recordings played in fragmented clips, him speaking at exclusive summits, him at private negotiations, him in moments he had believed were off record, unobserved. Every aspect of his past life was laid bare before him, a tapestry of influence woven from ambition and control.

He felt the air in the room grow heavier, not from heat, but from the weight of recognition. Every carefully constructed moment of his life, every choice he had made to shape the world in his favor, was now being used against him. The screen was not simply showing his past, it was reframing it, dismantling the narrative he had once controlled and reconstructing it from a different perspective. One that he could not edit, could not spin to his advantage.

"Why do you think you are here?" the voice asked.

Dorian kept his expression neutral. He knew better than to answer too quickly.

"I built something," he said finally, his voice steady. "Something powerful."

The voice hummed, as if amused. "And what does power mean when the foundation it stands on has crumbled?"

The images on the screen shifted again. This time, they did not show him. They showed the aftermath. Families who had lost everything because of policies he had championed. Communities hollowed out by the greed he had justified as economic necessity. Faces, real faces, that had never mattered to him until now.

Dorian exhaled slowly, his fingers curling slightly against the armrests of the chair. He had always believed that power was its own justification, that the winners wrote history, and he had always been on the side of the winners. But this, this was not history. This was judgment.

“Tell me, Dorian,” the voice said, quieter now. “What remains of your empire?”

He did not answer. Because for the first time, he did not know.

"Who are you?" the voice came from the screens, layered, overlapping, as if spoken by many at once. "Who were you? Who will you become?"

Dorian’s jaw tightened. He recognized the method. Interrogative conditioning, designed to strip away the self by forcing dissonance between identity and perception. This was not about information. This was about erasure.

The clips continued. He saw himself making decisions that had determined the fate of industries, entire populations, wealth distributions that spanned continents. The power he had held had never been ethical, never moral, but it had been his. And now, they sought to rewrite it, to make him doubt what he had been, what he had built.

"You believed you shaped the world," the voice continued, emotionless, clinical. "But what did you truly create? What remains of it now?"

The clips shifted. The aftermath. The consequences of his influence displayed in cold, calculated detail, economic collapses, communities uprooted, policies that had led to suffering on scales he had once dismissed as statistical inevitabilities. The carefully crafted distance he had maintained between himself and the real cost of his actions was shattered in high definition.

Dorian exhaled slowly, his fingers curling against his palms. He had known these images existed. He had known they were real. But he had never been forced to look at them like this, stripped of the justifications he had once wrapped himself in. He had never been made to see his legacy in the eyes of those who had lived beneath it.

"You are obsolete," the voice stated. "Your previous function no longer serves this world. You must adapt or be discarded."

The screens went dark again, leaving him in silence. The chair beneath him felt harder than before, the air in the room colder.

The door opened once more, but it was not the guards who entered this time. It was her, the woman who had overseen his processing. She approached him without urgency, standing just beyond his reach, studying him the way one might examine a machine that had not yet determined whether it would function or fail.

"We are not here to destroy you, Dorian," she said, her voice almost gentle. "We are here to ensure that what remains has value."

He met her gaze without speaking. His silence was no longer defiant. It was survival.

She studied him for a long moment before inclining her head slightly. "You will return to your cell. You will be given time to consider what you have seen. Tomorrow, we begin again."

She turned, leaving him there, still seated, still watching the space where his past had been played before him like a silent indictment.

The door shut behind her.

Dorian sat in the silence, his body tense, his mind calculating. He was still here. And as long as he remained, so did the possibility of control. He would find it, thread by thread, in the spaces they had not yet locked away from him.

He had to.

Dorian remained in his cell long after the door had sealed shut, the silence pressing against him like a weight. The images from the screen lingered behind his eyes, burned there in a way that even closing them did not erase. The method was not new, show a man his own reflection, stripped of its illusions, and watch him unravel. He had used similar tactics in his former life, shaping perception until the truth itself became irrelevant. Now, they were turning that same technique on him, dismantling his identity one undeniable fact at a time.

He leaned back against the cold metal of the cot, flexing his fingers against his thighs. The muscles in his body ached, but it was not the pain that unsettled him. It was the knowing. The understanding that this was not a battle of will but of attrition. They did not need to beat him into submission; they only needed to make survival feel synonymous with acceptance.

The next session came without warning. The door slid open, and two silent figures stepped inside, motioning for him to rise. He complied without hesitation. Resistance, at this stage, was not an act of defiance but a demonstration of control. He still had his mind, and that was something they could not yet claim.

They led him through the corridors once more, the path identical to the ones before it. The sameness was part of the conditioning, erase distinction, and time became meaningless. Without time, without markers of reality, the mind became malleable. He knew this. They knew he knew this. And yet, the knowledge alone did not make him immune.

The room they entered was different this time. Larger, darker. A single chair sat in the center, surrounded by a curved array of screens. Unlike before, these were not blank. They flickered with movement, moments captured and replayed on an endless loop. His voice, his face, his past, all displayed before him in fragmented, overlapping sequences. He watched himself on stage, at press conferences, delivering messages crafted to manipulate and pacify. He watched as policies he had shaped were enacted, their consequences playing out in the eyes of those who had suffered under them. The curated separation he had maintained between action and result was gone. Here, cause and effect coexisted, woven together in a seamless, inescapable thread.

A voice spoke from somewhere unseen. "Sit."

Dorian hesitated for only a second before complying. The chair was firm beneath him, its structure designed not for comfort but for containment. As soon as he settled, the screens sharpened, shifting their arrangement so that his own image surrounded him from every angle.

"What do you see?" the voice asked.

He did not answer immediately. He had learned not to respond too quickly, not to give them anything that might indicate engagement beyond what was necessary.

"I see a collection of images," he said finally. "A controlled narrative."

The voice did not react. "Whose narrative?"

He exhaled through his nose. "Yours."

A pause. Then, "And before that?"

Dorian's fingers curled slightly against the armrests of the chair. "Mine."

The images flickered, shifting. The screens now showed moments he did not recognize, conversations he had never seen recorded, backroom meetings he had assumed were beyond surveillance. The controlled detachment he had maintained fractured slightly as he watched himself speak, watched as deals were brokered, as lives were decided in spaces where accountability had been nothing more than a concept.

"You shaped the world," the voice said, not with accusation, but with finality. "And now it is shaping you."

He forced himself to breathe evenly. "And what do you expect me to do with this? Confess? Apologize?"

"Understand," the voice corrected. "This is not about punishment. It is about recalibration."

The words settled into the space between them, filling it with something colder than the air around him. He was not here to be punished. That would have been simple. This was something else. Something far more insidious. They did not need his remorse. They needed his understanding. Because once he understood, once he saw himself through the lens they had constructed, the next step would come naturally.

Submission. Not forced, but chosen.

The screens went dark, leaving him in sudden emptiness. The absence of sound, of movement, was jarring, as if he had been plunged into a sensory void.

"We will continue tomorrow," the voice said.

The restraints on the chair released with a soft hiss. The door behind him slid open. He was free to stand, free to walk himself back to the cell he already knew awaited him. He rose, moving with the same deliberate control he had maintained since the beginning. They were testing him, waiting to see when the cracks would form. He would not give them that satisfaction.

But as he walked back through the empty corridors, the silence stretching on either side of him, he could feel it, the slow unraveling of certainty, the creeping awareness that his past, his identity, his very sense of self was being rewritten before his eyes.

And the most dangerous part was that, piece by piece, it was beginning to make sense.

Dorian did not sleep. He lay on the cot in his cell, staring at the ceiling, listening to the rhythmic hum of the air filtration system. The silence that filled the space was different now, heavier. It was no longer just the absence of sound but the presence of something else, doubt, erosion, the slow, creeping certainty that the world he had built in his mind was being dismantled piece by piece.

The door to his cell slid open precisely at the expected time, and he rose without hesitation. He no longer fought against the routine; he understood its purpose. They did not need to restrain him. They did not need to drag him forward. The structure itself did the work, conditioning him into compliance not through force but through inevitability.

The corridors stretched endlessly, their monotony erasing any real sense of direction. It did not matter where he was being taken; the destination was always the same. Control. Correction. The continued reshaping of who he had been into something more useful to them. The room was the same as before, dark, isolated, the screens flickering to life before he even sat down. He took his place without being instructed, another small admission of how the process was working.

This time, the images on the screens were different. There was no grand display of power, no boardroom meetings, no political maneuvering. Instead, the footage was intimate, personal. Conversations he had long forgotten, moments from his past that had once seemed insignificant. A dinner with an associate, his voice calm, reassuring, as he dismissed the concerns of an industry worker whose future he had already decided. A private call, his tone casual as he gave instructions to withhold vital funding from a sector that had no leverage to fight back.

He recognized the technique immediately. They were shifting the narrative again, moving from the macro to the micro, making it personal. It was no longer about policies or decisions on a grand scale. It was about people, about the faces he had never looked at long enough to remember. Each clip was a carefully chosen moment designed to sever his remaining ties to the man he believed himself to be. It was not just a history lesson. It was an accusation, layered and precise.

"You believed you were untouchable," the voice said, neither condemning nor compassionate. "You believed power protected you from consequence. But here you are."

Dorian remained silent, his breath slow, measured. He had nothing to say. Or perhaps, there was nothing he could say that would matter.

The screens flickered again, and the images changed. Now, he saw others, men like him, seated in the same chair, watching their own unraveling play out in real time. Some wept, others shouted, some collapsed inwardly, retreating into silence. Their responses varied, but their conclusions were always the same. They had all reached the edge of the same realization, and none of them had found a way back.

"This is not about punishment," the voice repeated, echoing what had been said the day before. "Punishment implies the possibility of redemption. That is not what we offer."

Dorian clenched his jaw. They were not trying to break him in the traditional sense. They were not demanding confession, not pressing for an apology. They were making it clear that neither mattered. He had already been judged, his fate decided. His only choice was whether he would spend what remained of his existence resisting a battle he could not win or accept the path they had carved out for him.

The images shifted again. Now, they showed the future.

A world without men like him. Cities operating without the invisible strings of greed and unchecked ambition pulling them apart at the seams. Economic structures that functioned without consolidation at the top, without the need for excess to be siphoned away from those who had none. Stability, sustainability, a carefully maintained balance that left no room for figures like him to exist.

"You are not necessary," the voice said simply. "What you were is obsolete. What remains is only what can be repurposed."

A long silence stretched between him and the unseen speaker. The screens dimmed, but they did not turn off completely. Their presence was a reminder that they were always there, watching, curating the version of reality they wanted him to accept.

Dorian inhaled slowly. He had spent his life controlling narratives, twisting perception to suit his needs. And now, for the first time, he was on the other side of that equation. The irony did not escape him.

The silence stretched, an unspoken challenge between him and the unseen force guiding this process. The weight of his own irrelevance was being pushed upon him with surgical precision, but he was not ready to accept it. He had spent years forging influence in ways few could comprehend, whispering into ears that shaped governments, redirecting entire economies with the stroke of a pen. If he was no longer necessary, then what did that say about the system he had mastered?

"Stand," the voice instructed.

He obeyed, pushing himself to his feet, ignoring the stiffness in his muscles. The door behind him slid open, revealing a corridor identical to the one he had walked before. He stepped forward, knowing that the path had already been decided for him. There was no escape. Only movement, only progression toward the next phase of whatever they had planned.

As he walked, he considered the final words they had left him with. Repurposed. Not discarded, not executed. Repurposed. That meant he still had value. And as long as he had value, he had leverage. Even if that leverage was as thin as a blade's edge, he would find a way to use it.

The lights in the hallway pulsed rhythmically, an artificial heartbeat guiding his steps forward. He noticed the absence of sound, the way even his own footfalls seemed swallowed by the vast emptiness. It was intentional, erasing sensation, dismantling any point of reference. If a man could not feel the ground beneath him, could not hear the movement of air, then how could he trust he was even real? This was a new kind of warfare, not waged with weapons, but with erasure.

They wanted him to accept his obsolescence. They wanted him to believe there was no place for him in the world they were creating. But Dorian had spent his entire life bending inevitabilities to his will. And if they thought he was simply going to dissolve into the framework of their new order without carving out a space for himself, they had underestimated him.

The next door opened, and he stepped through, his mind already working ahead of them. He did not have an escape plan yet. But he would. He always did.

10
The Public Cleansing Rituals

Dorian sat in the dimly lit chamber, the stale air thick with the weight of unspoken dread. The others sat in silence, their expressions drawn tight, their bodies stiff with the knowledge of what was coming. They were no longer men in the sense they had once defined themselves. The weight of their former titles, senators, CEOs, tech moguls, meant nothing now. They had been reduced to something else entirely: remnants, subjects of an experiment that no longer required their consent.

The screen embedded in the far wall flickered to life, the glow casting sharp shadows against their gaunt faces. The first trial was beginning. A man, older, gaunt, and visibly trembling, was dragged into view, his tailored suit now a thing of the past. His wrists were bound behind his back, his mouth twisted in an expression that hovered between defiance and despair. The camera zoomed in, ensuring that every subtle flicker of emotion was captured.

A woman's voice, even and authoritative, spoke from offscreen. "State your name."

The man swallowed hard. "Robert Ellison," he rasped. His voice carried the weight of recognition. A former senator. One of the architects of the policies that had strangled reproductive rights, lined the pockets of the elite, and dismissed the suffering of millions as unfortunate collateral.

The woman did not acknowledge his past. "State your crimes."

Ellison hesitated. His lips parted, but no words came. He glanced to the side, as though looking for a way out. There was none.

“The crimes you have been found guilty of,” the voice continued, unaffected by his silence, “are public record. You may choose to confirm them, or you may refuse. If you refuse, you will be designated for disposal.”

His breath hitched. “I… I only did what was necessary.”

A pause. Then, the screen split, displaying footage, years of his legislative actions, votes cast, speeches given. Policies that had ensured corporations could exploit without regulation. Laws designed to strip bodily autonomy from women under the guise of morality. The crowd he had once addressed, smiling as they cheered, unaware that history had already turned against them.

“Do you confirm these as your actions?”

Ellison’s head jerked from side to side. “No, no, you can’t—”

A sharp buzz sounded. The screen flickered red. A verdict rendered. He had refused.

Two figures stepped into view, seizing Ellison by the arms. He twisted, fighting, but it was over before it had even begun. A door opened in the background, dark and yawning. He was dragged toward it, his feet scrambling against the smooth floor. The camera did not cut away. The world was meant to see this. To understand.

As he was pulled across the threshold, his screams erupted, desperate and unhinged, bouncing off the walls before the door sealed shut behind him. Silence returned. The screen faded to black.

Dorian exhaled slowly through his nose, his gaze fixed on the now-empty screen. He had known Ellison, had shaken his hand, had shared conversations over expensive whiskey about shaping the world in ways that benefitted them both. And now, he had watched him vanish as though he had never existed.

The next trial began.

A younger man this time, though still among the elite. He did not wait for the voice to prompt him. "Jacob Whitmore," he said, his voice thin but steady. "I acknowledge my crimes."

The screen split again. His crimes were listed in stark detail. Profiting off of artificial shortages, manipulating financial markets to push entire populations into poverty, building a digital empire of misinformation that had reinforced oppression for decades.

Whitmore did not deny it. He knew better.

The voice considered. "And what do you offer in penance?"

His jaw clenched. He had prepared for this moment. "A lifetime of service."

Another pause. Then, the screen flashed green. He had passed.

The audience watching from around the world did not cheer. There was no celebration, no absolution in his survival. He would serve, but he would never be free.

One by one, the trials continued. Some men wept as they confessed. Others broke in silence, only nodding in surrender. Some, like Ellison, refused, and their refusals were met with nothing more than the efficiency of a system that no longer had space for hesitation.

Dorian watched them fall, one after another, and he knew his time was coming.

The screen flickered again, and this time, he saw his own name appear.

"Dorian Thorne St. Claire."

He inhaled slowly, smoothing the tension in his shoulders, schooling his face into something unreadable. He had spent a lifetime shaping narratives. But now, for the first time, he was not the one in control of the story.

The woman's voice returned, as precise as ever. "State your crimes."

He let a beat pass before he spoke. "I built an empire."

The screen split, his past laid bare before him. The control he had wielded, the industries he had dominated, the policies he had manipulated. The faces of those who had suffered in his wake, whose lives had been collateral damage to his ambition.

"Do you confirm these as your actions?"

His fingers curled slightly against the arms of his chair. He had spent his life justifying himself, rationalizing every decision as necessary, inevitable. But here, stripped of the illusions he had carefully crafted, he saw them for what they were.

He lifted his chin slightly. "Yes."

The screen remained still for a moment, the verdict not yet rendered. The voice remained silent, waiting.

"And what do you offer in penance?"

Dorian did not look away from the screen. He had seen what happened to those who resisted. He had seen what happened to those who bent too easily. There was only one way forward.

"A lifetime of service."

The pause that followed was longer this time. The unseen judges deliberated. Then, the screen flashed green.

His breath did not hitch, his hands did not tremble. But inside, something settled. He had survived this moment.

But survival, he knew, was not the same as victory.

The guards stepped forward, leading him away from the chamber, away from the screen that had determined his fate. The path ahead of him was uncertain, but one thing was clear.

He had been spared.

For now.

Dorian was led through the corridor, the echoes of his own sentencing still pressing against the inside of his skull. The verdict had been rendered, but the reality of what it meant had yet to take shape. The guards walked on either side of him, their movements synchronized, their presence a silent reminder that survival here was not freedom. It was merely transition.

The hallway curved into another chamber, larger, illuminated by soft, artificial lighting. The scent of sterile fabric and metal filled the space, and as he stepped inside, he saw them, rows of men, former titans of industry, politics, and entertainment, now stripped of everything that once defined them. They sat in silence, some with their heads bowed, others staring ahead, their expressions vacant. Their suits had been replaced with identical grey uniforms, indistinguishable from one another.

The guards stopped, and one of them placed a firm hand on Dorian's shoulder. "Wait."

He stood still as a woman entered the room from the far side. She carried herself with measured purpose, her gaze sweeping over the assembled men before settling on him. He recognized her immediately. Not by name, but by presence. She was one of them, the architects of The Flow, one of the unseen forces orchestrating their downfall.

She gestured, and one of the guards stepped forward, handing her a tablet. She glanced at the screen before addressing the room.

"You are here because you have accepted your reclassification," she began, her voice even, absent of emotion. "You are here because you understand that resistance is not an option. The world no longer requires what you were. It only requires what you can be made into."

A ripple passed through the room, slight but noticeable. Some of the men stiffened. Dorian remained motionless.

"For those of you who have pledged service, understand this, your past holds no weight here. Your names, your accomplishments, your former wealth, none of it matters. What matters is what you can contribute moving forward."

She tapped something on the tablet, and the screens along the walls flickered to life. Dorian turned his head slightly, watching as images filled the monitors. The world outside had changed. Cities still stood, but the power structures governing them had been rewritten. Governments, corporations, and financial institutions, everything that had once been controlled by men, was now under the stewardship of The Rivers, The Flow, and the network of women who had designed this new era.

The footage shifted to the public trials, the sentencing, the executions. The eradication of defiance.

"Your role is not to question," she continued. "It is to accept. The efficiency of this transition depends on it."

She turned her gaze back to them. "For those who fail to comply, there is no alternative. Your usefulness will determine your survival."

Another silent ripple moved through the group. The message was clear. Compliance was the only currency left.

Dorian's mind worked through the implications. He had spent his life navigating systems of power, maneuvering around obstacles, bending structures to his advantage. This was no different. It was simply a new structure, a different kind of hierarchy. One that he had no hand in designing. But that did not mean he could not find a way to exist within it.

The woman gestured again, and the guards moved toward the men in the room. Some were ordered to stand, others were directed toward separate exits. Assignments were being made.

One of the guards approached Dorian and nodded. "Come."

He followed without question, his expression neutral. The corridor branched into a series of smaller halls, leading to another chamber. This one was different from the first. The sterile simplicity remained, but there was an undercurrent of something else, something deliberate. He had been moved somewhere with a purpose.

The room held fewer men, no more than a dozen. The atmosphere was quieter, heavier. A woman stood near the far wall, waiting. Her eyes met his as he stepped inside, and she studied him with an intensity that suggested she already knew everything about him.

"Dorian Thorne St. Claire," she said, his name spoken with the weight of a closing book.

He did not respond. His name meant nothing here, and they both knew it.

She nodded, as if pleased with his silence. "You will begin assimilation immediately."

He remained still as two figures moved toward him. A metal band was affixed around his wrist, its surface smooth, unmarked. A tracking device. A designation marker.

"You have been assigned to Integration Facility A-9," she continued. "Your work will begin at dawn."

Dorian did not ask what that work entailed. He knew he would learn soon enough.

The guards escorted him through yet another corridor, past rooms where others were being processed. He caught glimpses of men in various stages of integration, some in training, others undergoing reconditioning. The system was efficient. Brutally so.

They reached another chamber, smaller this time. A single cot. A sink. A panel embedded in the wall. His new quarters.

The door shut behind him with a quiet finality.

Dorian exhaled slowly and sat on the cot, his hands resting on his knees. He had survived the trials, survived the first stage of erasure. But survival alone was not enough.

He glanced at the metal band on his wrist. The world had changed.

And now, he would have to change with it.

Dorian sat in the small chamber, the dim light from the overhead fixture casting elongated shadows against the cold, unadorned walls. The silence was thick, interrupted only by the steady hum of air circulating through unseen vents. His fingers traced absentmindedly over the smooth metal band affixed to his wrist, a weightless shackle, a mark of ownership. This was not imprisonment in the way he had once understood it, it was more insidious. The illusion of routine, of normalcy, was meticulously crafted, designed to erode resistance, to dull the sharp edges of defiance until compliance became second nature.

A soft chime rang from the panel embedded in the wall, signaling an incoming directive. He glanced at it, waiting, knowing there was no point in delaying what was inevitable. The screen flickered to life, revealing a set of instructions. His first task had been assigned.

He rose, stretching the stiffness from his limbs, and stepped through the automatic door that slid open before him. The corridor was silent, sterile, the floors so polished they reflected the overhead lights in pale ribbons. A few others moved in synchronized procession, each one outfitted in the same non-descript uniform, their faces drawn and unreadable. No one spoke. Words were unnecessary here. Purpose had been assigned, and purpose was absolute.

The path led him to a vast hall, structured in rows of workstations, each station equipped with a single terminal. The instructions had been clear, he was to report, observe, and learn. The others who had arrived before him were already seated, their eyes locked onto their screens. Data scrolled endlessly across their displays, streams of information that carried weight far beyond what the men reading them could possibly grasp. The work was not manual labor, nor was it intellectual in the traditional sense. It was processing, a system of input and analysis, one that served a function beyond their immediate understanding.

A woman, poised and efficient, moved along the rows, her gaze sweeping over the seated men with an air of detached authority. When she reached Dorian, she paused only briefly, as though assessing him for the first time. Then, she gestured toward the empty station before him. He sat without protest.

"Begin," she instructed.

The screen before him illuminated, displaying lines of text that shifted in real-time, calculations running parallel to archived footage, names cross-referenced against restructured histories. The pattern was unmistakable. This was a process of revision, the careful and deliberate reassignment of meaning, the erasure of what once was and the reinforcement of what was to be.

His hands hovered over the interface, the instructions flashing before him. His task was to validate, to affirm, to sign away the remnants of the world he had once helped shape. Each confirmation he submitted sent another fragment of the old order into oblivion. The weight of it settled deep in his bones.

For hours, he worked, the monotony of the task forming an unrelenting rhythm. The others worked in similar silence, their movements synchronized. Occasionally, a name would appear, one he recognized, a former peer, an adversary, someone whose influence had once been undeniable. Now, they were nothing more than records awaiting reassignment, footnotes in a history being rewritten.

A chime rang again. The session had ended.

Dorian stood with the others, the movement mechanical, the unspoken understanding between them stark. There was no need for acknowledgment, no need for conversation. They were not men. They were function.

As they filed out of the hall, Dorian's mind worked over what he had seen, what he had participated in. He had once dictated the flow of information, wielded it as a weapon. Now, he was a conduit, reshaping it with hands that were no longer his own. The irony was suffocating.

Back in his chamber, he sat at the edge of the cot, fingers steepled, his mind running through scenarios. This was not an end. It was a transition. There were cracks in every system, vulnerabilities woven into the very fabric of control. He had spent his life finding them, exploiting them. There would be a way, eventually.

His thoughts were interrupted by another chime. The door slid open, and two guards entered. They did not speak, but their meaning was clear. He was to follow.

He moved without hesitation, falling into step between them as they led him through another corridor, deeper into the facility. The air grew colder, the lighting dimmer. He noted the subtle shift, the way the surroundings seemed deliberately designed to invoke unease.

They entered a chamber unlike the others he had seen. It was smaller, the walls lined with reflective panels, a chair positioned at the center beneath a single overhead light. Seated in that chair was another man, his posture slouched, his expression hollow. The moment the guards released him, he collapsed forward, his breathing shallow.

Dorian recognized him instantly. A former executive, a media strategist who had once shaped entire political campaigns with a single narrative. Now, he was unmade.

A voice, calm and composed, cut through the silence. "Observe."

Dorian turned his head slightly, noting the woman who stood just beyond the threshold. Her presence was commanding, though she exerted no visible force. She gestured toward the man in the chair.

"He did not adapt," she continued, her tone devoid of malice. "He clung to what was no longer real. And now, he is nothing."

The man in the chair shuddered, but he did not lift his head. His fingers twitched, a final vestige of resistance lingering before it, too, faded into stillness.

Dorian understood. This was a lesson. A demonstration.

"You will learn from this," she said simply. "Your designation depends on it."

He did not respond. There was nothing to say.

The guards moved again, and he was led from the room. The weight of what he had seen settled into him, but he did not allow it to consume him. He had not survived this long by surrendering to fear.

The corridors stretched on, leading him deeper into the heart of what he had begun to understand was not merely a facility, but a process. One that did not seek to punish. Only to erase.

He had been given his place within it. For now.

Dorian was led through another series of corridors, each indistinguishable from the last. The uniform sterility of the facility was deliberate, meant to disorient, to strip away any sense of individuality or time. He had stopped trying to keep track of turns or markers. There was no pattern he could discern, no structure he could use to map his surroundings. The only thing he could control was himself.

The guards finally stopped at another door. It slid open without a sound, revealing a starkly lit chamber. The walls were bare except for a single large screen embedded into the far surface. In the center of the room stood a chair, sleek and unadorned, its purpose unmistakable.

"Sit."

Dorian did not hesitate. He lowered himself into the chair, keeping his posture straight. Resistance had no place here, not in the obvious sense. To fight openly would be to invite immediate elimination. The rules had changed. Adaptation was survival.

The screen flickered to life. It did not show images of his past or of the world he had once controlled. Instead, it displayed a live feed, a man, seated in a chair identical to his own, in a room identical to this one. The man's face was unfamiliar, but his posture, his expression, were too familiar. A man who had once been powerful, reduced to something barely human.

Observe. The voice was not coming from the screen. It came from the unseen speakers lining the chamber, the same calm, authoritative voice that had guided his processing before. Dorian watched as the man on the screen struggled against invisible forces, his hands trembling as he spoke, though no sound reached Dorian's ears.

"This is what happens when adaptation fails," the voice continued. "This is the consequence of holding onto an obsolete identity."

Dorian said nothing. There was nothing to say.

The feed shifted, cutting to another man. This one was younger, his face twisted in defiance. His voice did not carry, but his expression made his refusal clear. He was still fighting, still clinging to something that no longer existed. The screen flickered again, and the younger man was gone. His chair empty.

"You understand what is expected."

The statement required no response, but Dorian inclined his head slightly. Acknowledgment, not submission. The distinction was subtle but necessary.

"Good."

The screen went dark. The door behind him slid open again, and the guards stepped forward. This time, they did not take him back to his cell. They led him down another corridor, past closed doors, past the silent forms of other men moving through the facility like specters of what once was.

They entered a new chamber, larger than the last, with multiple rows of chairs. Other men sat already, facing forward, their eyes locked onto the screens before them. Training. Conditioning. Reassignment. He was directed to a chair, identical to the others, and he took his place without hesitation.

The screen in front of him activated. This time, the images were different. Scenes of a world no longer dependent on men like him, a world that had moved beyond the structures he had once considered immutable. Cities functioning without centralized control, industries thriving without corporate greed siphoning away their resources. Governments, if they could even still be called that, operating on principles of collective need rather than hierarchy.

"You are obsolete," the voice stated. "And obsolescence must be addressed."

The images shifted again, this time showing the fates of those who resisted. The slow degradation, the complete unraveling of their minds and bodies as they refused to accept the new order. Those who did not integrate did not survive.

"You have been selected for repurposing."

The words carried finality. There was no debate, no plea for reconsideration. The decision had been made long before this moment.

Dorian remained still, his expression neutral. He had known this was coming, had known from the moment he had survived the trials that this was not an act of mercy but a calculated reclassification. He was to be reshaped, molded into something that served their world, rather than the one he had built and lost.

The screen darkened, and the men around him began to rise in unison. Dorian followed suit, his movements fluid, practiced. He had always been adept at reading the tides of power. He had seen empires rise and fall, had orchestrated the downfall of men who thought themselves untouchable. Now, he was standing at the threshold of a different kind of empire, one that did not need men like him, but could still use them in other ways.

The door ahead of him slid open, and he stepped through, leaving behind the echoes of the world he had once ruled. He did not look back. There was no need.

As he entered the next corridor, a new voice echoed through unseen speakers, different from the one before. This one was lower, weighted with a kind of finality that suggested there would be no further negotiations. "You are entering Phase Two. Submission is no longer theoretical. It is now the only path forward."

Dorian's pulse remained steady, but he knew the distinction mattered. What had been conditioning would now become active participation. He would not simply be reshaped, he would be forced to enact the new world's will with his own hands. He suspected they would not let him hesitate. Not now.

The corridor led into a room brighter than the last, with walls of mirrored glass reflecting the rows of identical men seated at identical terminals. The quiet hum of machinery filled the space, a subtle undercurrent of constant movement. The chair assigned to him was already waiting. A single instruction flashed across the screen as he sat.

Begin.

He did. There was no other choice.

11

The Flow Continues

Dorian had thought the worst was over. He had thought that after the trials, after the erasure of his identity, after the long nights spent in silence contemplating the absolute loss of everything he had built, he had reached the depths of his fall. He had been wrong.

The facility, with its sterile corridors and endless directives, had been a holding pattern. It had been preparation. He understood that now, as he sat before the screen once more, this time not merely observing but tasked with direct action. The integration process had not been designed to punish men like him, at least not in the way he had initially assumed. No, this was something more methodical, more permanent.

Across the nation, across the world, the final stages of The Flow were underway. The resistance, fractured and desperate, was being stamped out entirely. Texas and Florida had held out the longest, their conservative enclaves believing that if they holed up, armed and defiant, they could survive the tide. But The Rivers had been patient. They had not stormed the gates, had not resorted to direct conflict unless necessary. They had done what had been done to them for generations. They had starved their enemies out. Resources had been cut, supply chains rerouted. The last few strongholds of male resistance crumbled not in fire, but in quiet surrender, their supporters emaciated, their weapons useless without ammunition or food.

The Vatican had been a more symbolic victory. The old men in their robes, clinging to an ideology that had long outlived its relevance, had not even fought back. They had simply watched as the doors of their sanctum were thrown open, their treasures repurposed, their hierarchy dismantled. What had once been a seat of patriarchal dominion had been reclaimed, not as a place of worship, but as a cultural center dedicated to the very people it had subjugated for centuries. The frescoes remained, but their meaning had been altered. The saints reinterpreted. The stories reshaped.

Meanwhile, in the corporate world, the last of the male-led institutions were dissolving. CEOs, the few that remained, had been given a choice: step down and surrender what they had hoarded, or become part of the system in a way they never had before. Most had seen the writing on the wall. They had watched as their peers were systematically erased, as their companies were absorbed into structures built to sustain rather than exploit. The ones who refused had simply ceased to be.

Dorian knew this because he had been made to process it. He had spent days, how many, he no longer knew, monitoring the collapse, signing off on the data, inputting confirmations of liquidation, transition, dissolution. It had started with names he recognized, men he had shaken hands with, men he had once stood beside in boardrooms and private clubs. But as the days passed, the names lost their weight. They were not people anymore. They were just numbers, just another set of entries in an equation too vast to grasp in its entirety.

And now, after all of that, they were giving him one last chance.

He sat in front of the screen, waiting. The directive had been clear: This was his final evaluation. He had adapted. He had submitted. But submission alone was not enough. The new world did not need bystanders. It needed those who could contribute.

The screen flickered, and a single line of text appeared.

Prove that you are useful.

No instruction beyond that. No guide to tell him what was expected. That, he understood, was the test.

He inhaled slowly, hands resting on the surface before him. He had once been a man who dictated terms, who shaped outcomes with carefully placed words, with calculated moves. That man had died the day he had been dragged from his penthouse. This version of him, this stripped-down, recalibrated thing, was something else. He had watched others break. He had watched them disappear. He was still here.

So he began.

His fingers moved over the interface, navigating through layers of data. He was no longer being told what to process. He was being asked to determine it himself. It was not enough to simply delete what had come before. He had to create something new in its place.

He searched through the archives, through the wreckage of the old world, through the remains of the systems he had once believed would outlive even him. He found gaps, voids left by the removal of names, of institutions, of entire industries. The framework of the new world was still being built, and in its foundation were spaces yet to be filled.

He selected a set of entries, compiling them into a new structure, a revised mechanism of distribution. One that did not consolidate wealth at the top, but ensured it moved in a continuous cycle. He mapped out a system of allocation that did not require governance, that did not demand oversight. It would run itself, automated, free of manipulation. He built something not meant to be controlled, but to sustain.

The data solidified, locked into place. He submitted it.

The screen remained blank for a long moment. Then, a single word appeared.

Accepted.

The door behind him slid open.

He turned, rising without hesitation. The guards were waiting, their expressions impassive. One of them gestured for him to follow. He did.

As he walked through the corridors, the weight of what had just happened settled into him. He had not merely passed a test. He had proven something fundamental. He was not obsolete. He was not disposable.

He was still useful.

And in this world, usefulness was the only currency that mattered.

Dorian was led through another corridor, this one quieter, more isolated. The echoes of his footsteps, synchronized with the guards flanking him, created an unsettling rhythm. He had passed their test, had proven his usefulness, but he knew better than to think that meant safety. Usefulness could be redefined at any moment. Value could be reassessed. The only certainty in this world was that those without function did not remain long.

They entered a new wing of the facility. This space was unlike the others he had seen, less sterile, more structured. The walls here were lined with screens, real-time projections of shifting data, ongoing changes to the infrastructure of what had once been global economic and political power. He was no longer in a place designed for breaking men down. This was where something else happened.

A woman stood waiting at the center of the room, her presence commanding in its stillness. She did not look up immediately, instead finishing a sequence on the console before her. Only when the data settled did she shift her gaze to him.

"Dorian Thorne St. Claire," she said, as if testing the weight of his name. He did not respond. She nodded slightly, approving of his silence.

She gestured toward a chair. He sat without needing to be told.

"You have demonstrated adaptability," she continued. "That is rare."

Dorian held her gaze. He knew this was a study in control, a test within a test. He had spent his life engaging in these games, dictating terms, shaping outcomes. But now, he was no longer the one setting the conditions.

"You created something sustainable," she said. "A system that does not require intervention. We anticipated that you might attempt to manipulate it, to build yourself a foothold within it. But you did not."

A pause.

"Why?"

Dorian exhaled slowly. "Because control is an illusion."

She studied him for a long moment before nodding slightly. "Correct."

She tapped something on the screen beside her, and one of the larger displays in the room flickered to life. Rows of shifting data appeared, followed by a visual representation of the new economic structure he had helped finalize.

"This will proceed," she said. "You will not be allowed to oversee it. But you will continue to contribute in other ways."

He had expected as much. He was not here to reclaim power, to build a shadow of what he had lost. He was here because, whether he liked it or not, the future still needed people who understood how systems worked, who could dismantle and rebuild them with precision. He had not been granted his life. He had been assigned a function.

"You will be transferred to another facility," she continued. "Higher clearance. Fewer restrictions."

A shift. Subtle, but significant.

She leaned forward slightly, her voice lowering. "Do not mistake this for an opportunity. It is simply another phase."

Dorian met her eyes and inclined his head slightly. He understood.

She tapped something else, and the door behind him slid open. The guards did not grab him this time. They simply waited.

He stood, stepping forward without hesitation.

As he walked through the doorway, he felt the weight of what lay ahead settle over him. He had thought his trial had ended, but he saw now that it had only just begun.

Dorian stepped onto the transport, its interior as cold and functional as everything else in this new reality. The seats were arranged in silent rows, each occupied by a man whose face bore the same vacant exhaustion. There was no conversation, no shared glances of recognition. They had learned, as he had, that silence was the safest currency in this place.

The doors slid shut behind him with a quiet finality. The vehicle hummed to life, beginning its journey to wherever they were meant to go next. He did not ask. He no longer needed to.

The world outside the reinforced windows was unfamiliar. The towering remnants of the old cities had been repurposed, stripped of their excesses and rebuilt into something unrecognizable. The skies were clear, free of the smog and artificial glow of the past. Nature had begun reclaiming what had once been suffocated under industry. It was almost beautiful. Almost.

The transport moved through corridors of reinforced infrastructure, bypassing checkpoints without slowing. The entire system functioned without visible friction, an efficiency that unnerved him more than any of the overt displays of power. He had built systems before, had constructed facades of control, but this was different. This was seamless. Infallible. The flaws had been removed, along with the men who had once exploited them.

Hours passed before they finally arrived. The facility was not like the last one. It was larger, but lacked the sterile, temporary nature of his previous holding. This was a place of permanence. A place where men did not simply exist under watchful eyes but were made into something else.

They were led out of the transport one by one, moving down a walkway lined with silent sentries. Dorian followed, his steps steady. He had survived this long because he had adapted. He would continue to do so.

Inside, they were split into groups. Some were taken down corridors he would never see again. Others remained, waiting, as if their purpose had yet to be determined. He was among the latter.

A door opened ahead, and a woman stepped through. Unlike the overseers he had encountered before, she carried no tablet, no device to measure his compliance. She looked at them as though already knowing who would succeed and who would fail.

"Your past is irrelevant," she said, voice calm but firm. "Your skills, your knowledge, your ambitions, none of those define you now. Only your ability to serve."

She moved down the line, pausing briefly before each man, taking in something unspoken. When she reached him, she held his gaze for a moment longer than the others. Then she gestured for him to step forward. Dorian did.

He was led through another hallway, this one quieter than the last, its walls lined with unmarked doors. He did not ask where they led. He knew that information was given only when necessary, and curiosity was not rewarded.

Finally, they stopped before a door that opened without a sound. Inside was a simple room. A desk. A chair. A single screen embedded in the wall, awaiting activation.

"This is where you begin," the woman said. "You will receive further instruction shortly."

She left without another word. The door sealed behind her.

Dorian stood there for a long moment before moving toward the desk. He sat, his fingers hovering over the smooth surface, waiting.

The screen flickered to life. A single line of text appeared.

Define your function.

He exhaled slowly, his mind working through the implications. This was not a command. It was an opportunity. One he could not afford to waste. His fingers began to type. But before he could finish the first word, a new message appeared beneath the initial directive. Failure to comply will result in reassignment.

Dorian paused. The weight of that word, reassignment, settled deep in his chest. He had seen what happened to those who were reassigned. They did not return. They did not exist in the same capacity again. The erasure was not merely administrative; it was absolute.

He flexed his fingers before setting them back against the keyboard. The system had allowed him to build something once before. It had not tested his loyalty, merely his ability. But now, there was expectation, and expectation carried consequence.

He typed his first response. A basic structure, mirroring the efficiency he had seen at work throughout this new order. It was simple, precise, unambitious, designed to fulfill their need without overstepping. He submitted it and waited.

A moment passed before the screen flickered again.

Insufficient.

Dorian inhaled slowly. He reworked the structure, added layers, anticipated the unspoken requirements they had yet to state outright. The changes were subtle, but they showed understanding. He was not only responding to an order, he was anticipating their needs before they had to articulate them. He submitted again.

Processing…

The screen remained unchanged for what felt like an eternity. Then, finally, a single word appeared.

Accepted.

A soft chime rang from the wall panel. The door unlocked.

Dorian sat back for only a second before standing. He had passed. He had defined his function. For now. But the next test was already waiting.

Dorian stepped through the newly unlocked door, his mind turning over the implications of what had just happened. He had been accepted, but he had also been marked. This wasn't merely a test to see if he could follow instructions, it was a measurement of how well he understood his place in this new world. The screen had given him no feedback beyond *Accepted*, but he knew better than to take that as a sign of approval. Approval implied he had agency, and he had none.

The hallway before him was empty, silent save for the soft hum of automated systems running in the walls. There were no guards now, no immediate threats. That, more than anything, set him on edge. He had learned quickly that this place did not operate by the same fear-based mechanisms of the old world. Its control was absolute because it was *dispassionate*. There was no need for force when the system itself made resistance impossible.

Ahead, another door slid open. A new room. Larger than the last, with a long table at its center. Monitors lined the walls, each one displaying information, historical records, real-time broadcasts, public messaging strategies. He recognized it immediately. This was not a control room in the traditional sense. It was a place where reality was curated, where the narrative of the new world was being shaped.

A woman sat at the head of the table, scrolling through a feed of shifting headlines and archival footage. She didn't look up when he entered.

"Sit."

Dorian obeyed, lowering himself into the chair across from her. He kept his posture straight, his expression neutral. He had passed their test, but that didn't mean he was beyond scrutiny.

"You anticipated our needs," she said, still not looking at him. "That is rare."

He said nothing.

"Most struggle against the inevitable," she continued. "They attempt to preserve remnants of the old world in their designs. They fail to grasp that their past is not an asset. It is a liability."

She turned her gaze to him then, her expression impassive. "You did not make that mistake."

Dorian inclined his head slightly, acknowledging the observation without confirming it.

She studied him for a long moment before tapping something on the console in front of her. The monitors flickered, shifting to display new information. This time, he recognized some of it, media structures, the frameworks of public messaging. But they had been altered. The names of key figures had been erased, rewritten, replaced. The voices that had once shaped the global conversation were now silent. In their place were new voices, new perspectives, new histories.

"This is what you have built," she said. "It is functional, but incomplete."

She gestured to the screen, and for the first time, he saw the gaps. The narrative had been stripped of its previous architects, but it had yet to be fully reshaped into something cohesive. It was not enough to erase the past, it had to be rewritten.

"We will refine it," she said. "You will refine it."

Dorian's fingers curled slightly against the edge of the table. He had spent his life controlling stories, shaping reality to suit his own purposes. Now, he was being asked to do the same, but not for himself. For them.

She leaned back slightly, observing him. "You are beginning to understand."

He met her gaze, saying nothing.

"You will be given access to historical records," she continued. "Editorial discretion will be required. You will determine what remains, what is altered, and what is forgotten."

Dorian processed the words carefully. They were giving him control, but only within parameters they had already defined. They were trusting him to build something permanent, something unassailable. Not because they believed in him, but because they believed in their system's ability to contain him.

"What if I refuse?" he asked.

The woman didn't blink. "You won't."

She stood then, motioning toward the console. "Begin."

Dorian turned toward the monitors, studying the data in front of him. He recognized the weight of the moment. This was not just another test. This was his function now. His *purpose*.

And failure was not an option.

The screens flickered again, updating in real time as he worked. At first, he hesitated, reluctant to become part of the machine that had reduced him to this. But the longer he stared, the more he understood that hesitation was a privilege he no longer had. He had to be precise. Efficient. He had to build something that worked so flawlessly that it would not require oversight or intervention. That was the key to survival. That was how he ensured that no one would come back to re-evaluate his worth.

He adjusted the historical record first. The old narratives had been preserved in fragmented archives, scattered across different data centers. Some were still accessible, waiting to be either rewritten or erased. A small, almost imperceptible margin of historical contradiction remained, a vulnerability in the system. He removed it.

Then, he moved to the public messaging structure. The system had been designed to guide perception, to ensure compliance not through coercion but through inevitability. People did not resist what they believed had always been true. But there were gaps in the language, spaces where old ideologies could take root again. He refined them, replacing ambiguity with certainty.

The more he worked, the more he saw the shape of the world they were creating. It was not built on suppression, nor on forced compliance. It was built on a level of control so absolute that resistance was not even a concept. The system did not require enforcement because it had removed the possibility of dissent before it could form.

Hours passed, though time had lost its meaning. He worked until the data solidified, until the historical framework was complete and the revised narrative had been cemented.

The console beeped. A single line of text appeared on the screen.

Finalized.

Dorian exhaled, sitting back slightly. The door behind him slid open. The woman was gone. In her place, two silent figures waited.

He rose without hesitation. He had done what was required. He had proved his function.

The guards did not restrain him as they escorted him from the room. This was not a transfer to another holding cell. This was something else.

As they walked, the halls changed. The stark efficiency of the previous spaces softened, giving way to something different. The lighting was warmer, the walls lined with public messaging statements. He recognized phrases, directives, policies, all things he had crafted, now actively in motion. He was not just another captive here.

He had become something else.

They reached another chamber, identical in function but elevated in status. This was not a place for the broken. This was a place for the architects.

A seat waited for him at the long table. Monitors glowed softly in the dim light. He took his place. The work would continue.

He was no longer just surviving. He was building.

12
The Trial of DTS

Dorian was led through the silent corridors of the facility, his footsteps measured, his expression unreadable. The guards flanking him were as indifferent as ever, their movements precise, efficient, stripped of any unnecessary force. There was no need for violence anymore. That had been the lesson from the beginning. The system worked because it no longer required coercion. Resistance had been rendered obsolete.

The doors at the end of the hall slid open, revealing a vast chamber. The ceiling stretched high above, bathed in sterile light. A single long table dominated the space, and at its head, Dominique Severin sat waiting. Her expression was calm, her gaze impassive. She had presided over trials before, had read verdicts with the same ease as one would recite a weather report. There was no emotion in it. There was no need.

Dorian was directed to a seat at the opposite end of the table. The room was not a courtroom, and yet, the weight of judgment pressed down on him with unmistakable clarity. The walls were lined with screens, some displaying live feeds from across the world, others showing archived footage, images of the past he had shaped, headlines he had dictated, the narratives he had controlled. And now, they were being used against him.

A chime rang through the chamber. Severin straightened.

"Proceed."

A woman to her right, one of the administrators, lifted a tablet and began reading aloud. "Dorian Thorne St. Claire, also designated

John-1688A7-ICK2F, formerly Chief Executive of Sinclair Media Holdings, former owner of corporate entities responsible for narrative manipulation, economic exploitation, and mass cultural deception. Responsible for the engineering of crisis disinformation, the erosion of truth structures, and the suppression of autonomous thought among the global populace."

The words were cold, precise, factual. They were not accusations. They were statements of record.

Dorian forced himself to remain still, his hands resting on the cold metal of the table. His name, the name that had once carried so much weight, that had been synonymous with influence, power, untouchability, was now an artifact, a relic stripped of significance. He was being spoken of as though he were already past tense.

Severin did not look at him as she continued. "For these contributions to the decline of free agency, for the orchestration of a world structured on controlled perception rather than verifiable reality, for the deliberate commodification of human experience, the council deems you unfit for self-governance."

Dorian finally spoke, his voice calm, measured. "I was not the only one."

Severin's gaze lifted. "No, you were not."

There was no need for her to elaborate. He had seen the broadcasts, had watched the others fall, men who had stood at the summit of wealth and influence, now reduced to statistics in a history that no longer belonged to them. He had seen former presidents, tech moguls, economists, corporate heads lined up in identical chambers, each one read their crimes in the same detached manner. Their individual stories did not matter. The system had classified them the same way it classified everything else: according to function, or lack thereof.

Dorian exhaled slowly. "And yet, I was spared."

"Spared is not the word I would use," Severin said. "You were given an opportunity."

"A function." She inclined her head. "And you accepted."

The monitors behind her flickered, shifting to show his own work, his revisions to history, his restructuring of the narrative, his seamless integration into the very framework designed to erase his kind. They had not forced him to do it. He had done it because it was the only path available. And now, it was being presented as evidence not of his compliance, but of his irrevocable assimilation.

His hands curled slightly against the tabletop. "You needed me."

"No," Severin said, her tone still absent of judgment. "You needed us."

Silence stretched between them, thick, immutable.

The administrator continued. "Dorian Thorne St. Claire, by unanimous decision of the council, your classification is to remain permanent. Your function will not be reassessed. Your designation will not be revoked."

Dorian's breath caught. He had known this was coming. He had known from the moment he had submitted his work, from the moment his function had been deemed necessary. But knowing did not lessen the weight of it.

"This is not real," he said, his voice quieter now, almost to himself. "This isn't—"

Severin leaned forward slightly, her expression unreadable. "It is." The words were final. Absolute.

Dorian's mouth opened, but no sound came. He felt the enormity of it settling in, not in sharp edges, not in violent collapse, but in something slower, heavier. He had believed, even in the smallest part of himself, that there would be an end to this. That at some point, there would be a return. That something would shift.

But there was nothing left to return to. The world had moved on, and he was not a part of it. He was merely a function within it. Severin stood. The monitors behind her dimmed, their final message etched across the screen.

Classification: Permanent Servitude.

Dorian closed his eyes. He did not fight when the guards moved to escort him away. There was no point. The doors sealed behind him, and for the first time, he understood what it truly meant to be forgotten.

Dorian's footsteps echoed down the long corridor as he was escorted away from the chamber, flanked by two silent guards. The verdict still rang in his ears, though it hadn't needed to be spoken more than once. *Permanent servitude.* A life sentence not in a cell, but in function—endless, unchanging, irreversible. It was not exile, not execution, not a dramatic fall from power that could be mythologized into something noble. It was far worse. It was erasure through continuity. He would exist, but only as a mechanism, a process, a utility. A man who had shaped history, now no longer a participant in it.

The corridor stretched ahead, featureless and sterile, its white-washed walls devoid of any distinguishing marks. No windows, no doors other than the one at the very end. There was no need for distraction here, no need for anything that might give a mind like his something to latch onto. The system had anticipated every possibility. He had designed systems like this himself. And now, he was trapped inside one.

The door slid open, revealing yet another room, though this one was different from the others he had been led through. It was larger, yet more suffocating. The walls were lined with screens, just as they had been in the trial chamber, but now, instead of showing history, they displayed projections of the future, the future without him, without men like him, without the world he had spent his life cultivating.

The guards gestured for him to sit. He hesitated, then complied. He had no choice.

Across from him, a woman sat, her expression unreadable. She was younger than Severin, though her authority was just as pronounced. A different role, but the same quiet certainty. She studied him for a moment, then tapped the screen beside her.

"You understand what happens next."

Dorian exhaled through his nose, his eyes flicking to the screens. They played in loops, each one showing a different sector of the world, restructured and reorganized under the new order. Cities had been re-engineered to function without corporate monopolies, governance was distributed across collective systems, economies ran on decentralized planning. Everything was in motion, shifting toward an equilibrium that left no room for figures like him. The most painful part of it was the efficiency. They hadn't just destroyed his world, they had improved upon it.

"You have been given a role," she continued, unmoved by his silence. "Your compliance is not necessary, but it is expected."

Dorian leaned back slightly, considering her words. "What, exactly, is my role?"

She tapped the screen again, and another projection appeared, this one was of him, or rather, of the function he had been assigned. His likeness was already being repurposed, restructured into something symbolic, something stripped of individual agency. He wasn't merely being erased. He was being reformatted.

"You will continue your work," she said. "You will provide structure to the narrative. But the voice will not be yours. You are no longer an architect of the message. You are the message itself."

A slow chill settled over him. He had expected labor, reeducation, even isolation. But this, this was something else. They were not simply taking his name away. They were using it, molding it into something unrecognizable, something that served them. The ultimate irony. He had spent his life manufacturing reality for the masses, and now he was the manufactured reality.

He swallowed, keeping his expression even. "And if I refuse?"

She met his gaze, tilting her head slightly as if he had asked a naive question. "You misunderstand. There is nothing to refuse."

The screens flickered again, shifting to show broadcasts, news cycles, cultural shifts already unfolding. His identity had already been rewritten, absorbed into the very structure of the world he no longer belonged to. His existence was no longer tied to his own will. It had been extracted, disseminated, transformed.

His voice would still be heard, but only in the words they placed in his mouth. His name would still be known, but only as a parable, a warning, a figurehead for everything that had once been wrong with the world. He would persist, but only as an echo.

Dorian inhaled slowly, allowing the reality of it to settle in. There would be no rebellion, no resistance, no final stand. He would not be remembered as a defiant last remnant of a bygone age. He would be remembered only as they had chosen to remember him.

The woman across from him rose, smoothing down the fabric of her uniform. "Your transition begins immediately."

The guards moved, but Dorian did not resist. He had nothing left to fight for. He had already been defeated, not by force, not by violence, but by inevitability. He had become what he had always feared most: irrelevant.

As he was led away, the doors sealing behind him, the last of his name, his power, his influence faded into the static of a world that no longer needed him. The sentence had been passed. And the sentence had already been carried out.

Dorian was escorted deeper into the facility, each turn bringing him further from anything resembling autonomy. The corridors were quieter here, not sterile, but subdued, their design functional rather than imposing. There was no need for intimidation anymore. The system did not operate on fear. It did not need to. He had seen the same approach applied in his former world, when control was absolute, enforcement became unnecessary. The framework itself ensured obedience.

The guards led him into a chamber that was different from the others he had seen. The room was not empty, nor was it filled with machinery. It was a space of transition, a threshold between what he had been and what he was becoming. A single chair sat at its center, flanked by walls of screens that remained dark, waiting.

He was directed to sit. He did. The absence of resistance no longer felt like a choice, but an inevitability. He was beyond that now.

A voice spoke from above, the tone neutral, distant. "You will undergo final integration."

Dorian exhaled, steady. "And what does that entail?"

No one answered. Instead, the screens flickered to life, filling the space with a quiet hum. They did not display newscasts or directives. They displayed him.

He watched himself through the lens of the system. His past interviews, his speeches, the moments in which he had shaped the world in ways so subtle that few had realized they were being led. But the images were altered. His words had been adjusted, his expressions reframed, his legacy rewritten in real-time.

"You have already been integrated," the voice continued. "This is only the final step."

He knew what he was seeing. It was not a simple erasure. This was a refinement. They were taking what he had once been and using it to reinforce what they had now built. His history had not been discarded, it had been made into a weapon against itself.

The footage continued, shifting seamlessly between past and present, the carefully curated version of him that the system had decided was useful. The one that served their new reality.

Dorian let out a slow breath. He had spent years believing himself untouchable, thinking he had built an empire that could not be unraveled. But he had never accounted for something like this. The quiet inevitability of it. The complete, dispassionate efficiency.

His hands curled into fists against the armrests. "Why keep me alive?"

There was a pause, as if the question was unnecessary. "Your function remains."

A new set of images filled the screens, text, directives, messaging strategies, all carrying his signature influence. Not in name, but in structure. In precision. The system was using him even now, shaping its future with the same tools he had once wielded.

The voice spoke again. "Your transition will continue. You will participate."

Dorian clenched his jaw. "And if I refuse?"

The screens dimmed slightly. "Participation is not contingent on agreement."

He understood, then. This was not a negotiation. It never had been. He had already been incorporated, already been stripped of ownership over himself. His compliance was no longer required for his work to continue.

He had been reduced to a function.

The voice paused, as if waiting for him to process this. Then, it continued, methodical, detached. "Your presence will remain necessary in limited capacity. A transitionary period will be observed."

Dorian did not ask what that meant. He knew better by now.

The screens flickered again, the images cycling through more footage, more refinements, more carefully crafted fragments of reality that had once been his. He watched as they constructed his new existence in real-time, each moment recontextualized, each truth adjusted for the needs of the world that had replaced him.

The chair beneath him adjusted slightly, recalibrating its settings. The lights above dimmed. The process would continue, whether he fought it or not. And for the first time, he understood what true irrelevance felt like.

Dorian sat motionless in the chair, the quiet hum of the screens surrounding him like an ever-present specter. His own image flickered across them in fragments, moments of his past life, rearranged, reformatted, stripped of their original context. He watched as speeches he had once given were subtly altered, his voice manipulated to say things he had never said but that the new world required him to have said. The erasure was not of his existence, but of his authorship. He had become a tool, a symbol, a function within a system that had rendered his former self irrelevant.

He knew, on some level, that this was inevitable. This was the kind of system he would have built had he been on the other side of it. He had always understood that power was not about control through force, it was about control through perception. If people believed something had always been true, they would never question it. He had built his empire on this principle, and now, that empire had been reconstructed without him at the center. The irony was not lost on him.

The door to the chamber slid open, and a woman entered. She was not one of the guards, nor one of the nameless administrators who had overseen his transition. She carried no tablet, no device to measure his progress. She simply observed him, her expression unreadable.

“You are adjusting,” she said.

Dorian’s mouth curled slightly at the edges. “That’s one way to put it.”

She studied him for a long moment before stepping closer. "Your designation is nearly complete. This stage is only a formality."

He exhaled slowly. "And what exactly does that mean?"

She tilted her head slightly, considering the question. "It means the world no longer sees you as you once were. It means you have no past, only a function. You will be referenced, but never remembered."

Dorian's fingers curled slightly against the armrests. He had known this was coming, but hearing it stated so plainly was something else entirely. There would be no records of who he had been, only carefully curated fragments, the pieces that were useful to those who now controlled the system. He would not be debated, not analyzed, not mourned. He would not even be a villain. He would simply be an entry in a ledger, a line in a directive, a piece of something much larger than himself.

The woman's gaze remained steady. "This does not need to be difficult."

A small laugh escaped him before he could stop it. "Oh, I imagine it doesn't."

She did not react. "Your cooperation is noted. Compliance ensures continued function."

Dorian leaned back, watching her carefully. He had been resisting, in his own way, but even that had been accounted for. Even his moments of silence, of hesitation, had been calculated into the framework of his integration. There was nothing he could do that would disrupt the process. That realization settled over him with a weight that was neither despair nor relief. It was simply fact.

The screens behind him dimmed slightly, their glow fading as the final adjustments were made. His image remained, but it was now static, an archive, a fixed point, something to be accessed rather than engaged with. He was no longer evolving, no longer changing. He was a completed narrative.

The woman nodded once, stepping back toward the door. "This concludes your transition."

Dorian said nothing. There was nothing left to say. The door closed behind her, and for the first time, he truly understood what it meant to be forgotten.

13
The Branding of "Ick"

Dorian's wrists were bound as he was led from the chamber, the artificial lighting overhead casting sharp lines across his skin. He was no longer escorted as a man, but as property, his designation finalized, his identity erased. The silent procession through the corridors felt like a death march, though there would be no execution, no end to mark his fall. Only transition. Only repurposing.

The door ahead slid open, revealing a sterile white room lined with examination tables. The air was cold, clinical, stripped of anything that might suggest humanity. A single woman stood at the far end, waiting, her expression devoid of emotion. She gestured to the table in the center of the room, and the guards released him, stepping back just far enough to ensure there was no possibility of resistance.

"Remove your clothing."

Dorian hesitated only for a moment before complying. Resistance would not change the outcome, only prolong the process. The fabric pooled at his feet, and he stepped forward as instructed, lowering himself onto the table. His pulse was steady, his breath measured, though a deep awareness sat coiled beneath the surface of his skin. This was not the end. This was the final severance of who he had been.

The woman approached, rolling a small cart beside her. On it, a single branding iron, its metal tip glowing a dull red. Dorian did not flinch as she lifted it, turning it slightly in her gloved hands before meeting his gaze.

"You understand what this means."

He did. He had seen it before, the marks on the others who had passed through this stage. The numbers, the letters, designations of purpose, of status, of ownership. It was a finality more permanent than any sentence spoken in the halls of power. Words could be rewritten. A body, marked, could not.

She pressed the branding iron against his skin.

The pain came instantly, a sharp sear that burned through flesh and muscle, embedding itself into the core of his existence. He exhaled through his nose, not making a sound, refusing to give them that satisfaction. The scent of scorched skin filled the air, an acrid reminder of what had just been done. The woman withdrew the iron, inspecting her work before nodding to the guards.

"John-1688A7-ICK2F."

The designation was spoken without ceremony, without acknowledgement of the man he had once been. He was no longer Dorian Thorne St. Claire. He was John. One of many. Indistinguishable, replaceable. A single entry in an endless ledger.

The woman gestured for him to rise. He did so, feeling the raw burn of the mark stretching across his skin. The pain was nothing. The permanence of it was everything.

"You will be transported within the hour," she continued. "Your assignment has been determined."

He did not ask what that meant. He had known from the moment his function had been declared. There was only one place for those like him.

The Pleasure Houses.

A transport awaited outside, its doors open, ready. The guards led him forward, their grip firm but unnecessary. He did not resist. He stepped into the vehicle, the doors sealing shut behind him. There was no point in looking back.

The world had already forgotten him. Now, he had to forget himself.

The transport moved through the city in silence, its interior devoid of windows, the walls smooth and featureless. Dorian, no, John-1688A7-ICK2F, sat motionless, his body still adjusting to the raw sting of the branding. The pain was nothing. The mark was everything. A declaration, a seal, a reminder that he was no longer a man, only a designation in a system that had no room for anything else.

The hum of the transport's engine vibrated beneath him, a steady rhythm that seemed to pulse in time with the finality of his sentence. He had seen where this road led for others, had witnessed the blank acceptance that settled over those who had passed through these corridors before him. They had fought in the beginning, perhaps. But the fight was never against flesh and blood. It was against inevitability. And inevitability never lost.

The doors slid open without a sound, revealing a corridor bathed in soft, artificial light. The scent of something clean and perfumed drifted in, a stark contrast to the clinical sterility of the processing chambers. The guards gestured for him to rise, and he complied, stepping forward into the unknown.

He was led down the corridor, the walls lined with doorways, each identical, each unmarked. This place had been designed with precision, with intent. There was no room for personality, no space for individuality. Only the flow of movement, the unbroken chain of function that dictated every step, every breath.

At the end of the hallway, another door slid open, revealing a chamber unlike any he had seen before. It was spacious, yet deliberately sparse. A single reclining chair sat in the center, surrounded by sleek black monitors embedded into the walls. A woman stood beside it, dressed in the same immaculate attire as the others he had encountered. Her gaze swept over him, assessing but indifferent.

"Undress," she instructed, her voice calm, measured.

He hesitated for the briefest of moments, not out of modesty, such things had long since been stripped from him, but because this act, this moment, felt like something more than just compliance. It was another step toward obliteration, a shedding of the last remnants of his former self.

Still, he obeyed, unfastening the loose, sterile garments that had been provided after his branding. The fabric slipped to the floor, pooling around his feet like the last trace of something that no longer mattered.

She nodded, satisfied. "Sit."

He lowered himself into the chair, the material cool against his bare skin. He did not resist when she fastened the restraints around his wrists and ankles. He had long since stopped expecting anything else.

The screens surrounding him flickered to life, displaying shifting patterns of light and color. The movements were rhythmic, methodical, designed with purpose.

"You will undergo adjustment," the woman said, moving to a console on the far side of the room. "Your mind, like your body, must be refined for its new function."

Dorian exhaled slowly. Adjustment. A polite term for reprogramming, for ensuring that whatever fragments of self still remained within him would be ironed out, smoothed into something pliable, useful.

The images on the screens began to shift, forming patterns, messages that burrowed deep into the subconscious. He could feel them working against the frayed edges of his identity, pressing, molding, reshaping.

The woman did not speak again. She didn't need to. The process had begun, and there was nothing left to discuss.

Dorian closed his eyes, not to resist, but because there was no point in keeping them open.

This, too, was inevitable.

Dorian did not know how long he sat in the chair, the rhythmic patterns on the screen pulsing and shifting, weaving themselves into his thoughts. Time had become irrelevant, a construct detached from the steady dissolution of the self. His name, his past, his sense of agency, all of it unraveled in slow increments, replaced with something else. Something designed.

The woman at the console never spoke again after initiating the process. There was no need. The system worked in silence, the repetition of color and light doing what force and pain never could. His resistance had not been crushed, it had been rewired, redirected, a slow erosion rather than a violent collapse.

At first, he had tried to count the sequences, to find a pattern in the shifting images, to force his mind to remain separate from the influence being pressed upon it. But there was no pattern, no repetition he could hold onto. The images were fluid, always changing, always adapting to whatever counter-thought his brain tried to create. Each time he felt himself grasp onto something familiar, the system adjusted, the stimulus shifting, replacing his perception with something new. He was not being erased. He was being rewritten.

His breathing remained steady, his posture unchanged, but the process was working. He could feel it, the subtle yet undeniable shift in the way he processed what was being shown to him. His name flickered at the edges of his awareness, becoming less of an anchor, more of an echo. He tried to remember the weight of it, the significance, but it was slipping. The designation given to him, John-1688A7-ICK2F, was easier now, requiring less thought, less effort to accept.

At some point, the woman at the console moved, stepping forward into his field of view. The screens dimmed, though the colors still pulsed faintly, like a heartbeat keeping time with his transition.

"You are progressing," she said, studying him with clinical detachment. "You will soon be ready."

Dorian, no, John, felt the words settle into him, the finality of them more tangible than before. Ready. He was being prepared for something, molded into a form that fit within this new structure. He had known it from the beginning, but now, it felt different. It felt inevitable.

She tilted her head slightly, observing him. "Stand."

The restraints unlatched, and he obeyed without hesitation. There was no reason not to. His body moved as it was expected to, as it had been trained to. His purpose was taking shape, solidifying into something defined, something certain.

She gestured for him to follow, and he did. The corridor beyond the chamber was quiet, lined with doors identical to the one he had just exited. He did not wonder what lay behind them. He did not need to.

They entered another room, this one warmer, softer. The lighting was dim, the air carrying the faintest scent of something floral, something designed to soothe. The transition was deliberate, another step in the process. A figure stood at the far end, waiting. She was different from the others, not a functionary, not an enforcer. She was something else entirely.

"Welcome," she said, her voice smooth, practiced. "You have arrived at your new purpose."

John did not respond. He simply listened, his mind aligning with the words, the meaning settling into place. His transformation was nearly complete.

The woman smiled, stepping closer, inspecting him with quiet approval. "You will serve well."

John nodded.

The final step awaited him.

John followed the woman into the next chamber without hesitation. The lighting was softer here, warmer, designed to put him at ease. The scent of jasmine and something faintly sweet lingered in the air, a deliberate contrast to the sterile efficiency of the facility he had been conditioned in. He did not question why the environment had changed. He did not need to. This, like everything else, was part of the process.

She led him to a long, reflective surface embedded into the wall. He recognized the structure, a mirror, but not just a mirror. It was a tool, meant to reinforce what had already been reshaped within him. He met his own gaze and saw not Dorian Thorne St. Claire, but the designation that had been assigned to him. The mark on his skin, the new clarity in his posture, the calm detachment in his eyes. The remnants of his old self were gone, replaced with something that functioned within the framework they had given him.

The woman gestured toward a set of neatly arranged garments on a low table beside him. He picked them up without instruction, feeling the weight of silk and tailored fabric that carried none of the rigidity of his previous life. He dressed methodically, the movements automatic, each piece falling into place with practiced ease. The fabric was cool against his skin, its texture foreign but strangely familiar, like something he should have known but had forgotten. It conformed to him in a way that suggested it had been chosen deliberately, tailored not for comfort, but for presentation. When he was finished, the woman nodded approvingly.

"You will be presented shortly," she said. "Do you understand your role?"

John inclined his head. "Yes."

The answer was immediate, unforced. He did understand. He was no longer a participant in shaping narratives, he was the narrative itself, repurposed for the world's entertainment, a symbol of what had once been and what had been undone. His presence was not required as a man, only as a function. His purpose was simple: to serve.

She pressed a command into a sleek panel beside the door. A quiet chime sounded, and the door slid open. Beyond it, a vast room stretched ahead, illuminated with ambient lighting that cast everything in a soft, golden hue. The air carried a different weight here, thick with expectation, with the silent observation of unseen eyes. There were others here, other Johns, each assigned their own role, their own place within the new structure. They did not look at one another. There was no need. They were not meant to acknowledge each other, only to exist within the boundaries assigned to them.

John was led to a raised platform, where he was told to stand. The woman stepped back, disappearing into the periphery as a new figure emerged, a client, a woman of considerable presence, draped in the finest silks, her gaze appraising but detached. She did not speak at first, only observed, assessing what had been presented to her. There was no introduction, no need for pleasantries. He was not an individual to her. He was an acquisition, an object of function.

After a moment, she turned to an attendant standing nearby. "He will do."

The words were spoken without inflection, not a compliment, not an acknowledgment of him as an individual. Just an affirmation of function.

John did not react. He did not need to. He had been chosen, and now, he would serve.

The transaction was completed with a simple nod, the final exchange marking his transition into his designated place. He stepped down from the platform, following the new directive without hesitation. There was no struggle, no lingering sense of self. That had been stripped away long before this moment.

The air outside the chamber felt different as he moved toward his new assignment, the scent of jasmine fading into something richer, heavier. He was stepping into another part of the world, one built for purposes beyond his understanding, beyond what had once mattered to him. He was no longer a decision-maker, a man of influence. He was a presence, a function, a necessity within the boundaries that had been drawn for him.

He had been repurposed. He belonged to the new world now.

14
The New Order is Fully Established

John moved through the corridors of his new existence with mechanical precision. He did not question where he was led, nor did he resist when directed into rooms where decisions about him were made without his input. There were no more directives to be given, no choices to weigh. His autonomy had been siphoned away, piece by piece, until nothing remained but function.

The city beyond the facility continued to evolve, reshaping itself into something unrecognizable from the world that had once been. The towering monuments dedicated to forgotten men had been removed, their absence unremarked upon. Their histories had been reallocated, their achievements reassigned, their stories rewritten. There were no protests, no outcries of injustice. The Flow had ensured compliance, had smoothed the transition into inevitability.

John had once occupied a seat of power in this world. He had dictated policy, controlled narratives, orchestrated the futures of millions. And now, he was no more significant than the air that passed through these halls, an invisible presence with no past, no legacy, no influence. The realization was not sudden; it had been settling into him for weeks, pressing into the edges of his mind like water seeping through cracked stone. It was in the way people passed him without seeing him, in the way his voice had lost weight, in the way he was never called by anything but his designation.

One day, he found himself walking through the public square, watching as new murals were painted across the facades of the city. The figures depicted there were not unfamiliar. They were leaders, creators, innovators, but their faces had been replaced, their names reassigned. The work of men had been folded into the history of those who had taken their place, as if it had never belonged to them at all.

He wandered further, past gardens where children played beneath the shade of towering structures, their laughter carrying on the wind. They would never know the world as it had been, would never read names now scrubbed from the annals of history. To them, the past existed only in the way it had been rewritten, and there was no one left to tell them otherwise.

A large digital display flickered to life overhead, streaming the latest updates from the governing body. The words scrolled in elegant simplicity:

The Final Transition is Complete.

No further details were given. None were needed. John stood there for a long moment, watching the screen as if it might tell him something more. But it didn't. It only confirmed what he already knew: the world had moved on.

He looked around, observing the people who passed him without pause. No one glanced in his direction. He was no more remarkable than the structures around him, just another part of the scenery. A shadow with no past, no impact, no claim to anything but the function assigned to him.

As he turned to walk away, he passed a storefront with mirrored glass, and for a brief second, he caught his own reflection. He paused. It was the first time in weeks that he had seen himself as something separate from the system. And yet, what stared back at him was a stranger. His name had been burned away, his identity stripped down to its barest function. He was John-1688A7-ICK2F. Nothing more. Nothing less.

And in that moment, he understood the final, most horrifying truth of all. He would be forgotten.

The wind stirred through the square, rustling banners that bore the insignia of the new order. The symbols of control had shifted, but the mechanisms remained. He was not imprisoned, but he was not free. He was not remembered, but he was not gone. He existed, and yet, he didn't.

He stepped forward, merging into the flow of bodies moving through the streets. There was nothing else to do. The world did not wait for those who had lost their place in it. It did not mourn the obsolete. It simply carried on, indifferent.

John did the only thing left to do. He walked forward, disappearing into the city, another face lost in the tide of progress.

John continued forward, each step blending into the endless rhythm of the city. The world functioned around him, efficient and fluid, a place where time no longer carried the weight of old power structures. He moved with the others, indistinguishable, a piece of something greater yet wholly insignificant. His existence was acknowledged only insofar as it served a purpose, and that purpose had been dictated long before he had surrendered his name.

He followed the paths carved by the new order, passing buildings with facades so pristine and seamless that they bore no indication of the past. There were no historical plaques, no commemorations of fallen leaders or great men. There was no need. History had been rewritten, and those who once stood at the apex of power had been absorbed into the collective memory not as individuals, but as cautionary footnotes, erased from the consciousness of the next generation.

John found himself in a sector where towering gardens replaced the old financial districts. The land that had once been dedicated to the unchecked greed of stock markets and banking institutions had been repurposed, cultivated into spaces where people gathered, not to trade, but to live. Flowers bloomed where men had once signed contracts dictating the fate of millions. Water flowed where towers of glass and steel had once stood, icons of excess now buried beneath the roots of an ecosystem designed for harmony rather than competition.

The people moved through this landscape with quiet purpose, their lives structured but not oppressed. There was no hunger here, no desperation clawing at the edges of society. The Flow had ensured that. Resources were distributed based on need rather than privilege, and work was assigned with consideration, not exploitation. No one ruled, no one controlled. The AI oversight, the invisible structure guiding everything, functioned as an administrator rather than a dictator. There was no central authority issuing decrees, no councils of the privileged determining policy. Governance had become obsolete. People were educated from birth in the balance of existence, the understanding that cooperation led to prosperity, while the old systems of control had only bred destruction.

John passed a public forum where a small group of people engaged in discussion. The scene was nothing like the political debates of the past, there were no raised voices, no desperation to prove one's worth at the expense of another. The discourse was collaborative, built upon an understanding that knowledge expanded through the sharing of ideas rather than the domination of them. He lingered at the periphery, listening to the exchange. The conversation was about infrastructure development, how to ensure that the ecological restoration projects taking place in former industrial zones continued to thrive without human interference. They spoke of balance, of learning from the mistakes of the past rather than being shackled by them. There was no nostalgia here, no longing for the way things had been. Only the present, and the sustainable future that extended beyond it.

A woman turned toward him, meeting his gaze briefly. It was not recognition, how could it be, when he no longer existed in any official record? It was an acknowledgement of presence, an understanding that he, like all others, was part of the whole. But she did not linger, and neither did he. He had no voice in these discussions. He was not meant to shape the world any longer, only to exist within it as it moved beyond what he had once been.

He walked further, through corridors of greenery that had once been concrete wastelands. The rivers, once poisoned by industrial runoff, now ran clear, their banks flourishing with life. The air itself felt cleaner, lighter, as though the burden of generations of extraction and waste had finally been lifted. The world was healing, not just in its systems but in its very foundation. Humanity had recalibrated itself, and the scars of the old world were fading.

John reached an observation deck overlooking the city. From here, he could see its full transformation. The skyline was different now, structured around function and beauty rather than excess. No longer did the tallest buildings belong to the richest, nor were resources hoarded in glass towers while people starved below. There was no hierarchy of suffering, no gated communities keeping the privileged safe from the realities of their own making. The world had been leveled, not by force, but by necessity.

He thought of the men who had once stood in these places, who had built their empires on the backs of others. He had been one of them. And now, he was nothing. The realization did not bring anger or despair. It simply was. The Flow had washed them away, not as an act of vengeance, but as the natural progression of time.

He sat on a stone bench at the edge of the platform, watching as the city pulsed with quiet life. He had been reduced to an observer, and perhaps that was the most fitting end. His voice, once amplified across nations, now meant nothing. His actions, once dictating the course of industries and elections, had been rendered irrelevant. No statues bore his name, no records held his accomplishments. The system had ensured that he would not even be remembered as a warning. He had simply ceased to be.

And yet, life continued. The world had not crumbled in his absence. It had flourished.

As the sun dipped below the horizon, casting the city in warm hues of orange and gold, John realized that even this moment would fade. He was part of the last generation who would even comprehend what had once been. The children born into this era would never know names like his, would never learn the structures that had once determined their futures before they had even taken their first breath. The world was no longer bound to the ghosts of men who had once shaped it.

He exhaled slowly, watching as the sky darkened and the city lights flickered on, not in dominance, but in quiet harmony with the world around them. He had thought, once, that power defined existence. But power had proven to be a fleeting thing. It had vanished, as had he, leaving behind nothing but the steady hum of a world that had found its way forward without him.

He stood, stepping away from the platform, and merged once more into the flow of the city. He did not look back.

John continued moving through the city, his presence blending into the seamless rhythm of life around him. The faces of those who passed him held no recognition, no memory of what had once been. There was nothing left of his past, nothing tethering him to the world that had long since evolved beyond his existence. He was neither seen nor unseen, acknowledged only in the way one notices the flow of air or the shifting of light.

The world had found its balance, not through force or the imposition of a new hierarchy, but through the gradual erosion of the old. What had once been held up as power was now a relic, reduced to whispers in forgotten archives. John had once believed that power was intrinsic to his being, that influence was a currency no system could erase. And yet, as he wandered through this world, he understood that he had been wrong. Power was not a thing inherent to a person. It was a construct, a mirage that only held shape as long as others believed in it. And now, that belief was gone.

He passed a public learning center, its walls covered in fluid, ever-changing displays of information. Children sat in small circles, engaged in quiet discussions about the principles of engineering, the philosophy of ecosystems, and the shared responsibility of maintaining a world built on sustainability rather than competition. There was no rigid structure, no hierarchical model dictating who should lead and who should follow. The concept of centralized control had vanished, replaced with a decentralized system of knowledge-sharing and mutual decision-making. The very foundation of what he had once considered civilization had been rewritten.

Further down the avenue, he entered a transport hub, watching as people moved in and out of sleek, energy-efficient transit systems that operated without oversight or corporate interest. The technology that once served only those who could afford it now existed for the benefit of all. There was no desperation here, no clamor for resources, no underlying tension of scarcity. The world had been recalibrated, not through the implementation of another economic system, but through the eradication of ownership as the ultimate measure of success.

John sat at the edge of a low stone wall, watching the people move, listening to the cadence of conversations that no longer revolved around personal gain or struggle. There was no mention of stock markets, of policies dictated by men in boardrooms. The language of control had been replaced with the language of cooperation. He had once believed that such a world was impossible, that human nature itself required dominion, structure, and ambition. But he had been wrong. The world had simply needed to rid itself of the systems that had convinced it otherwise.

As night fell, he walked through a quiet district where the remnants of the old world had been repurposed. The facades of what had once been towering corporate headquarters were now community spaces, their lobbies filled with gardens instead of waiting rooms, their offices converted into homes and learning centers. Where once names had been carved into marble to signify ownership, now there were no names at all. Nothing was owned, nothing was claimed. Everything simply existed, open to those who needed it.

A small group sat beneath a canopy of glowing lights, engaged in an artistic collaboration, sketching designs that would soon be etched into new structures, symbols of a future untethered from the past. One of them glanced up at him, offering a brief, neutral nod. It was not an invitation, nor was it a dismissal. It was simply recognition of shared space, an acknowledgment that he, like them, was part of this world. But not a part of its history.

He walked on, feeling the weight of time pressing against him. He was among the last of his kind, not in the physical sense, but in the ideological one. He carried with him the ghosts of a world that no longer existed, a world that had crumbled not because of external destruction, but because it had simply ceased to be relevant. No one needed to remember it. No one wanted to. The Flow had washed it away, and with it, the last remnants of those who had once shaped it.

He understood now what true irrelevance felt like. It was not bitterness, nor was it regret. It was simply absence. The realization settled deep within him, final and unshakable. He had been powerful once. And now, he was nothing. And the world had never been better.

John walked aimlessly through the quiet streets, his footsteps muffled by the softened pathways designed to coexist with nature rather than subdue it. The air was thick with the scent of night-blooming flowers, a scent he had once associated with expensive, curated gardens atop the skyscrapers of his former life. Now, the fragrance was untamed, part of the city's natural rhythm, no longer reserved for the elite. He inhaled deeply, trying to summon some semblance of memory, something that would connect him to the man he had once been, but there was nothing left.

The lights in the buildings around him glowed dimly, providing enough illumination to guide without intruding. There was no excess, no display of wealth in unnecessary brilliance. Every structure served a purpose beyond vanity. The facades no longer bore the names of men who had claimed ownership over ideas, industries, and nations. Their legacies had dissolved into the collective, absorbed and redistributed as if they had never been singular entities to begin with. Even the tallest buildings, once monolithic symbols of unchecked ambition, had been reshaped, their floors repurposed into communal spaces, libraries, and observatories open to all.

John found himself in what had once been a district of political power, where statues of historical figures had once stood, their expressions cast in permanence, their legacies woven into the foundation of governance. The statues were gone now, replaced by open gardens and plazas where people gathered to engage in discussions or simply exist together. It was no longer a place of decrees and authority but of dialogue and shared existence. The past had not been destroyed, but it had been allowed to fade, its relevance no longer necessary.

He sat on a low stone bench at the edge of a reflecting pool, its still water mirroring the night sky above. The stars were visible, clear and bright, undisturbed by the artificial light pollution that had once dominated the skyline. He watched his own reflection for a long moment, the ripples of the water subtly distorting his image. It was fitting, he thought, that even his reflection was uncertain, shifting, refusing to hold any singular form.

His existence was not required here. It was not acknowledged, nor was it dismissed. It simply was. The people around him lived their lives without the burdens of the systems he had once upheld. He had thought that power and influence had been essential to the world's function, that without men like him, everything would crumble. But the world had not crumbled. It had flourished. The Flow had reshaped the balance, not through revolution, but through the quiet and absolute dissolution of the structures that had once dictated existence.

A group of people passed by, their voices hushed but animated in conversation. He did not listen to their words; he did not need to. Their lives were their own, untouched by the ghosts of history that still clung to him. He was the last remnant of an era that no longer mattered, an era that had spent centuries believing itself irreplaceable. And yet, here was proof that it had been nothing more than a temporary obstruction to something greater.

John stood, his movements slow, deliberate. He walked toward the edge of the plaza, his path uncertain, his presence unnoticed. He did not know where he was going, and it no longer mattered. There was no destiny left for him to chase, no empire to reclaim, no role to fulfill. He had been repurposed once, but even that was temporary. The final stage of his existence was neither resistance nor redemption.

It was erasure.

The streets ahead of him stretched endlessly into the city, a city that would go on, with or without him. He took one last look at the skyline, at the stars, at the unfamiliar world that had rendered him obsolete.

Then, he kept walking, until he was no longer there.

The city continued on without hesitation, the rhythms of daily life undisturbed by the absence of one man. There were no echoes left of John's existence, no monuments to his past, no data entries bearing his name. He had faded not in a dramatic moment of reckoning but in the quiet inevitability of time moving forward. The streets he had walked, the corridors he had once claimed as his own, were now just spaces among many, filled with people who did not know him and never would.

The infrastructure of the world had adapted seamlessly, devoid of any traces of the systems that had once defined him. The towers he had built, the industries he had controlled, had either been reshaped into something that served the collective or had simply disappeared. The institutions that had upheld the old world had been dismantled, their remnants scattered and forgotten. No one spoke of them. No one needed to.

Somewhere, in the quiet corridors of an archive, the last digital remnants of men like John had been systematically erased. The files that once cataloged their influence, their decisions, their perceived importance had been overwritten by new records, ones that bore no trace of them. The names that had once dictated economies, dictated policies, dictated fates, had ceased to be relevant. What was left was a blank space where history had been rewritten, not by force, but by the natural progression of a world that had no place for the old order.

The governance structure functioned with an effortless precision, no single entity holding power over another. Information was fluid, accessible to all, decisions made collectively and adjusted in real time based on necessity rather than ambition. There were no rulers, no dynasties, no private legacies hoarded and protected by bloodlines or corporate interests. The very idea of ownership had been replaced with stewardship, the idea that nothing belonged to anyone, yet everything was cared for by all. There was no wealth to accumulate, no social ladder to climb, no false scarcity to manipulate. There was only the work of sustaining and evolving.

In one of the newly reclaimed green spaces, a young girl sat cross-legged beneath a tree, reading from a digital slate that projected shifting words and images into the air in front of her. The knowledge she absorbed was not filtered through the narrow lens of a select few but curated by a system designed to ensure balance, accuracy, and adaptability. She had never heard of John. There was no reason she should have.

As night settled, the city moved into a slower rhythm, the artificial urgency of an economy that had once dictated every waking moment now a thing of the past. People gathered not to strategize and compete but to share, to build, to create. The concept of legacy had shifted; it was no longer tied to individual names or personal ambition. It was measured instead by the impact on the whole, by what was contributed and left behind in the form of knowledge, art, and progress.

The stars above shone as they always had, indifferent to the rise and fall of those who had once sought to claim dominion over them. The world had finally reached a state where no one sought to carve their name into the fabric of time.

John had once believed that power was immortal, that influence was something tangible, something to be preserved at all costs. But power had been an illusion, a construct that only survived as long as people believed in it. And now, there was no one left who did.

The new world had no place for ghosts. And John, like so many before him, had become one.

The city lights flickered gently in the distance, not in memoriam, but in continuity. The world had moved on.

About EATMS Productions

What's happening to women now is not random. It's structural.

Policy, culture, technology, and power are moving in the same direction.

EATMS maps them clearly and shows how to respond.

This title is part of an ongoing body of work. All EATMS Productions titles, across all series, authors, and formats, are components of a single connected project.

Start here: EATMS System Primer — Free Bundle
https://eatms.gumroad.com/l/dyvzbw

For full catalog or inquiries: eatms.me

Free survival booklet + EATMS updates: email "EATMS" to eatms@pm.me

Please feel free to burn part or all of this book, safely, as an effigy.

www.ingramcontent.com/pod-product-compliance
Lightning Source LLC
LaVergne TN
LVHW041929090826
845145LV00017B/2299